Mehmet Murat Somer was born in Ankara in 1959. After graduating from the Middle East Technical University Industrial Engineering Department, he worked for a short time as an engineer, and for an extended period as a banker. Since 1994, he has been a management consultant, conducting corporate seminars on management skills and personal development. When not working out in the hammam, he writes books in the Hop-Çiki-Yaya series, of which *The Prophet Murders* is now one of six. He lives in Istanbul.

The Prophet Murders

Mehmet Murat Somer

Translated by Kenneth Dakan

A complete catalogue record for this book can be obtained from the British Library on request

The right of Mehmet Murat Somer to be identified as the author of this work has been asserted by him in accordance with the Copyright, Designs and Patents Act 1988

First published in Turkey in 2003
First published in the UK in 2008 by Serpent's Tail,
an imprint of Profile Books Ltd
3A Exmouth House
Pine Street
London EC1R 0JH

website: www.serpentstail.com

ISBN 978 1 84668 633 7

Typeset by FiSH Books, Enfield, Middx.
Printed by CPI Bookmarque, Croydon, CR0 4TD

10 9 8 7 6 5 4 3 2

The Prophets

Bünyamin	Benjamin
Ibrahim	Abraham
İsa	Jesus
Lut	Lot
Muhammet	Mohammed
Musa	Moses
Nuh	Noah
Salih	Salih
Yahya	John the Baptist
Yunus	Jonah
Yusuf	Joseph
Zekeriya	Zechariah

One

I grabbed a cup of coffee and the morning paper and settled into my chair by the window. It's my morning ritual. I drink only two cups of coffee a day. The first, always in the morning. Mind you, what I call "morning" is what ordinary people refer to as "the afternoon". I go to bed late. For I am, as they say, "a creature of the night".

A news item on page three hit me like a slap in the face.

"Transvestite Burned to Death".

I got a sour taste in my mouth. Naturally, it affected the flavour of my coffee: the last mouthful was distinctly bitter. Putting down my cup, I concentrated on reading the article. Bad news about our girls always gets me down. Not all of them enjoy a life of leisure like me. Some of them make a living out on the streets. It can make them tough and hostile.

For many reasons, the number of our dead is on the rise. Life gets more difficult with each passing day; petty crime is rife; our girls are growing careless; everyone's out of control and violence is spreading. The price of life is cheaper than ever. And as for our girls, they're getting knocked off for a handful of change.

Many of the girls working the highway have been hit-and-run victims. The sense of security they got from working in large groups turned out to be a false one. The end, when it came, was sudden. And bitter.

Just like my coffee when I saw the news.

This time, the tone of the tabloid was especially demeaning and nasty. Exactly what you'd expect from page three. As always, they ran an old picture of the victim as a man. In other words, someone less colourful and lively than the person we all knew. What's more, it was an unflattering picture from an identity card. A transvestite called Ceren. I didn't really know her; she didn't hang out at our club. Her real name was İbrahim Karaman. And she was only twenty-three.

I quickly scanned the report from start to finish. She died in a fire in her apartment in Tarlabaşı. Fortunately, no one else lives in the abandoned building. The fire company suspects faulty wiring or a smouldering cigarette butt.

Our girls have the survival instincts of wolves. They seem immune to disaster and can cope with just about anything. But like everyone else, when they're drunk or doped up they might sleep through a fire. That's probably what happened. I felt a sharp pang, thinking about how someone so young, in the spring of her life, had been cut down in her prime. Had she ever even fully savoured the joys of being a transvestite?

I tossed aside the paper and stared blankly at the street below. A series of images flashed through my mind: the faces of all the girls we'd lost. I can't think of a single transvestite who has died of natural causes. Foul play is always involved. And the police invariably record the deaths as unsolved crimes. If murder can't be proved, our girls are always blamed. That's how the press treated this particular case: a fire broke out in the home of a drunken vagrant, a stoned transvestite. And he died. I silently cursed them all. But it didn't help. I was still furious.

After a while, I forced myself to snap out of it. Life goes on, despite the pain. And I had a lot of work to do. Most urgently, I was due to have my legs waxed. Fatoş *abla* is an elderly transvestite. Before becoming too decrepit, and in order to avoid – in her words – "becoming a spectacle", she had taken up a new career. Fatoş *abla* goes from house to house, waxing shoulders, plucking eyebrows and even giving the odd hormone injection to those who require one.

I was born with shapely eyebrows. I have never resorted to hormones, and have no intention of doing so. I glory in being both Man and Woman. As for waxing...it is a basic and constant necessity.

Fatoş *abla* has the gift of the gab. Her clients roar with laughter as she regales them with tales of her younger days, then scream with pain as she uproots unwanted body hair. Even though I've been having my legs done for years, and my arms and bottom depilated on occasion, it still hurts every time, and my eyes always fill with tears. Fatoş *abla* teases "Well, it's not easy; all that manly bristle." While men with dark complexions have coarse hair, fair-skinned types like me are usually covered in down. At least, that's what I'm like. My light complexion may make me more sensitive to pain. Anyway, all I know is that I sometimes scream silently, and at other times like a banshee.

Fatoş *abla* rang the bell right on time. The older she gets, the less trouble she takes with her make-up and appearance. As a result, she looks strangely ordinary. If I passed her on the street, I'd describe her as a big woman with strong features. She was wearing a simple short-sleeved cotton dress, printed with large roses on a cream background. Draped over one shoulder was an enormous straw handbag, and on her feet were low-heeled leather sandals, one size too small. As always, her toes and heels overflowed. The effect was completed by an old-fashioned straw hat, trimmed with a swathe of fabric matching her dress. Her eyes were hidden behind oversized dark-tinted glasses. At one time, she no doubt paid a small fortune for them.

As she laid out the tools of her trade, I undressed. I chose some music to ease the pain and drown out my cries: a CD compilation of old Turkish pop hits that a friend made for me. Every half-remembered song from the late '60s and early '70s is there. I love singing along with the ones I remember the words to. Fatoş *abla* knows them all by heart, and dredges up long-forgotten showbiz scandals she has read about in the gutter press. Our session started off light-heartedly enough.

The first song is "Birazcık Yüz Ver (Pay a Little Attention to Me)", a rhythmic number by Gönül Turgut, someone I greatly admire as a woman, as well as an artiste.

Fatoş was off and running.

"Gönül Turgut was the greatest singer of her time, you know. Even Ajda Pekkan used to imitate her when she first came out."

"Whatever happened to her?"

"She gave up music when she got married. What a waste of talent. And a shame for music, too."

"She was an alto. Just like us," I threw in.

"How dare you!" she bellowed. "No one talks about my Gönül Turgut like that. How can you compare a foghorn to a voice like hers? Just listen!"

As she spoke, she stripped off another patch of hair, deliberately provoking a loud scream and deftly underlining her point.

We got idle chatter about singers and their lives out of the way. It was time to talk about the morning news of Ceren's fiery death. Fatoş *abla* had heard about it too. As she applied warm wax to my leg, she began:

"But Ceren never lived there. Her apartment's in Cihangir, near Taksim. Right behind the German Hospital. I waxed her legs often enough to know."

"What do you mean? That she didn't die at home?"

"That's what it looks like to me," she replied. "Like I said, her place was in Cihangir. Near Siraselviler. And certainly not in some derelict building on Tarlabaşı. And it wasn't abandoned. There are respectable people living on every floor. In fact, our girl Afet was living there. On the floor above."

My leg didn't hurt all that much, but when she moved up to my groin I started letting out regular shrieks. Fatoş *abla* paused to think for a moment. Then she corrected herself.

"I think she still lives there. She hasn't made any appointments, but I ran into her on the stairs last time I visited. She didn't even say 'hello".'

It was clear she looked down on standoffish Afet, but was it really fair of her to take it out on my groin? My eyes filled with tears.

"Don't worry about it," I groaned. "The world's full of insensitive people."

"I feel the same way. But what do I care if she ignores me? Am I the one who's still wet behind the ears?"

"These new ones have no manners or respect," I deliberately provoked her.

"Get her! Look who's talking? And how long have you been

around?"

We burst out laughing. But my groin still smarted.

We chatted about this and that. As the CD began playing "Anılar (Memories)", composed and sung by Uğur Akdora for Turkey's first Eurovision song contest trials, we paused for a glass of cold *ayran*. We agreed that it was one of the best songs in the history of Turkish pop. And sang along softly.

"That girl's disappeared too," I murmured.

"That 'girl' is the same age as your mother. And what do you mean 'disappeared'. She's splashed across all the society pages. I think she even writes a column for one of them."

"You mean Uğur Akdora landed a rich husband and gave up music, too?"

"Oh no, sweetie. Her family was well-off to begin with. She condescended to share her three songs with the people, and then reclaimed her place up there in society."

She waved in the general direction of the ceiling.

I was now silky smooth. Fatoş *abla* massaged lemon juice into the newly waxed areas, to prevent rashes and swelling.

Just as she was leaving, she got a puzzled look on her face. "It just doesn't make sense. What on earth was that girl doing in a deserted building? All by herself . . . And she was so choosy about customers and where she worked. There were entire neighbourhoods she'd refuse to visit, let alone a place like that. It doesn't make any sense. Anyway, may Allah grant a long life to the living," she concluded, sighing heavily as she made her way down the stairwell.

I realised I've overlooked something. And Fatoş *abla* had put her finger right on it. Seriously, what was one of our girls doing in a vacant building in the middle of the night? And all alone?

Two

What was Ceren doing in that abandoned building in Tarlabaşı? Assuming she had some sort of business, why on earth did she stay when her work was done? And why didn't she flee when the fire broke out? How did she burn to death?

I didn't have the answer to any of these questions. But perhaps I could find someone who did. I sat down next to the phone. First, I called Hasan. The head waiter at our club, he refers to himself as the "maitre de club". Despite working at a transvestite joint, Hasan isn't even gay. Not yet, anyway. At least that's what he claims, and we go along with it. None of us – not just me – know of his having ever been with a woman, man or girl. He's acquainted and on good terms with all our girls. You could say he was like our community *muhtar*, the elected, well-informed head of a village or neighbourhood. Hasan's up on the latest news, especially when it comes to who's been doing what with whom. In other words, he's got the goods on us all. And what he doesn't know, he immediately finds out. As you may have guessed, he's quite a character.

Clearly, he'd just woken up. No, he hadn't heard of Ceren's death. Yes, he was truly upset. No, he didn't really know her, had seen her just a few times with some of the other girls. She'd

been in great demand recently, and was willing to cater to the
more bizarre fantasies of her customers. She'd fallen out with
her neighbour, Afet, so I wouldn't be able to get much information out of her. She usually went hooking with a new girl, Gül.
No, Hasan didn't know much about her either. Yes, Hasan was
going straight back to bed when I got off the phone. No, it
wasn't that he'd finally had an amorous adventure of some
sort, it was just that a crying baby on the floor above had kept
him awake. We'd talk later at the club.

Although I wasn't able to find out what I was looking for, I
had managed to learn quite a lot about Ceren. And from
someone who didn't even know her well.

Despite what I'd been told, I decided it would still be worthwhile to call Afet. She is one of the girls who hang out at the
club, if only from time to time. Afet is quarrelsome and
malicious, and her long, aubergine-purple hair is teased up high,
in order to make her look taller. Unable to stand up straight on
her high-heeled shoes, she bends her knees slightly while
walking, which gives her an even more menacing appearance.

Picking up the phone, Afet immediately announced that she
was too busy to chat unless it was urgent, adding that she'd
come to the club early for a talk. We arranged a time.

Neither call had satisfied me. And there was still time to kill
before the game shows I'm addicted to. I went to my computer
room to do some surfing. First, I armed myself with a glass of
ice tea the size of a vase and some spinach *börek* I'd picked up
from the patisserie.

I love cooking, and am good at it, but just don't feel like
bothering these days. At most, I grill a cut of meat and toss a
simple salad. When dining out at a quality restaurant, I've got

no problem; but when it comes to snacking, I seem to gravitate towards whatever's labelled junk food. At this rate, everything in my wardrobe will have to be let out. So much for Audrey Hepburn elegance!

Internet chat sites seem to be growing more popular and crowded by the day. In addition to the standard sex rooms, there are ones for lesbians, gays and transvestites. I'm the webmaster of one of them. The room's called "Manly Girls"! There's a novel of the same name. Full of high hopes, I bought it in high school. But when it turned out to be a runny-nosed melodrama I abandoned it in a forgotten corner. The novel was a dud, but its title was perfect for us. In an inverted sort of way. I sometimes go online to chat or to monitor other conversations. If someone catches my attention – and someone inevitably does if I stay online long enough – I open up a private window.

The name of our chat room sometimes attracts aggressive trolls. They join in, cursing and threatening, until they're kicked out. The regulars agree that most of them are closet cases, as gay as can be. I could track them down and ban them for life, but they tend to sign-in from internet cafes or secretly from their workplaces, so it wouldn't do much good. They'd just find another way to come back.

For example, we've got a radical fundamentalist who goes by the codename Jihad2000. This person drops in at least once a night to warn us in capital letters that we're all doomed. That we're the reason the country has gone to hell, which is where we'll all burn for eternity. He claims it's blasphemy for us to recite prayers, since our foul mouths would only soil the word "Allah". After a couple of minutes, he's done. He storms into the room, interrupts everyone's chat, fires off his messages and disappears in a puff of fire and brimstone. Then he drops by again later if he's got nothing better to do.

I suspect that Jihad's nick refers to a holy war waged against us.

In other chat rooms, he's the perfect gentleman. If you respond in kind, he answers immediately. Then he starts boasting, telling you what a whiz he is when it comes to computer systems. Actually, he's not half bad. As long as he doesn't ask anything personal, I usually respond. He comes up with various cyber solutions, explaining how different programs can be used. And he never seems to tire of informing you how brilliant he is.

Because we both stick to the same nicks whenever online, we've developed a sort of virtual acquaintance. I can't say we're friends, but then again, who needs friends in cyber space?

As far as I can tell, Jihad2000 is a young, completely inexperienced and totally repressed closet homosexual. The girls sometimes egg him on, and then things really get going. I worry that one of these slanging matches will end with the site getting permanently shut down.

The second I got online, Jihad2000 appeared. He was in fine form. He had prepared all his messages in advance, ready to be floated in. So there was no way to respond. We were all quiet, reading what he'd written.

I skimmed through the list of nicks while waiting for his diatribe to end. I recognised a few names. Most of those in the room try to pass themselves off as super macho types. They choose names they think are provocative, or at least obscene. As I read through them, I kept an eye on Jihad2000's messages.

He was banging on about a transvestite who burned to death, who suffered the tortures of hell while still on this earth.

All eyes, I began concentrating. This was the first time he'd gone into such detail. He must have read about it in the newspaper, and been inspired.

(*written in red characters*)
<YOU SHALL ALL BURN. ROAST IN RED FLAMES!
PERVERTS
YOU HAVE STRAYED FROM THE PATH OF RIGHTEOUSNESS.
HAVE CHOSEN THE WAY OF SHIT
HELL AWAITS YOU!
THE INFIDEL WHO DIED TODAY WAS NOT THE FIRST
AND WON'T BE THE LAST!
HERETICS, PREPARE YOURSELVES !
A HOLY WAR HAS BEEN LAUNCHED!
YOU'RE NEXT!>

As always, his connection was cut as soon as he'd floated his message. Either one of our operators had kicked him out, or he'd bolted. I had too much on my plate to know which.

Thanks to Jihad2000, all hell broke loose. The room buzzed with panic. Those who hadn't yet witnessed his antics showered the others with questions. Who died? Where? When? How? Who did it? Were religious fanatics responsible? Were we all doomed? It took some time for chat to return to normal. Using my webmaster code, I took a look at what he'd written earlier. I'd only caught the end, and wondered what I'd missed.

<HERETICS, INFIDELS!
YOU ALL BLASPHEME .

YOU SEEK TO ALTER THE ALMIGHTY'S CREATION
DO YOU REALLY KNOW BETTER THAN THE GREAT
CREATOR?
YOU'RE ALL PERVERTS!
YOU'RE ALL DAMNED!
YOU WILL BE PUNISHED FOR YOUR SINS HERE ON EARTH!
ONE OF YOU WENT UP IN FLAMES!
THE SINNER IBRAHIM HAS BURNED!
THE WORLD HAS ONE LESS SINNER!>

The words really threw me. He'd gone too far. Why this hatred? Why this venom? I sensed a headache coming on.

One of the girls I know from the site opened a private window and asked me what was going on. I quickly summed it up for her. She hadn't read the papers, and became upset. Then vindictive.

I'd had enough, and it was clearer than ever that I faced a migraine. I switched off the computer and went to the living room. It was almost time for my game show.

I never get the slightest pleasure out of game shows. I'm just addicted. It's upsetting to realize how much more I know than the average contestant. Their lack of knowledge makes me cross; I curse their ignorant certainty. But I don't miss a programme. I suspect this is a form of masochism.

The first contestant was a young woman, an Istanbul University student. Her glasses, straight hair parted down the middle and drab clothes lent her an intellectual air.

As I munched on spinach *börek*, I let her have it with my best insults. I didn't expect her to hear. And if she had, what would she have made of me? I was on a roll. She was disqualified on the fifth question.

It concerned music terminology. She was asked to identify the odd one out from: symphony, sonata, opus and oratorio. Naturally, she wasn't aware that opus refers to the numerical chronology of a composition. She chose oratorio, and was neatly eliminated. My headache had worsened to the point where I require medication. I turned off the TV.

I took a painkiller, and then started concentrating on redirecting energy flows. Exercise is best for this. I'm practised in Aikido and Thai-boxing. As long as I'm not faced with an armed opponent, there's no one I can't handle. For this reason alone, the neighbourhood shows me a certain respect. No matter how frivolous or flamboyant my outfits, I'm considered an *abi*, a big brother.

After tackling one of a growing number of purse snatchers, my standing in the neighbourhood increased still further, and not just in the eyes of the rescued victim, Hümeyra Hanım, a woman banker.

I generally exercise in my guest room, which is usually empty. I prefer working out to music, but my throbbing head demanded otherwise. Physical activity and a rush of adrenalin would ease the pain.

I finished my standard warm-up routine. Then I moved on to mid-air kicks, first single, then double. With a good leap, I can manage three short jabs with the same foot. In rapid succession, it's enough to stupefy any adversary. With an even higher leap, my blows connect quite nicely with my adversary's head.

Next, I moved on to forward and reverse hits. It's easier when faced with an opponent. But you can't always get what you want. I made do, working at switching legs in mid-air, which I'm not so good at. Sometimes I lose my balance. I need more practice.

I worked out until I was gasping for breath and soaked in sweat. But no trace remained of that headache. I sprinted to the shower.

Having decided to go to the club early, I began to get ready. When I'm feeling low, I dress simply. That is, no make-up and absolutely no glitz of any kind. I was ready in no time.

I wriggled into a white jersey halter-neck I found among my mother's old clothes from the '70s. Teamed with a red patent leather mini-skirt, it made me look like the Turkish flag. Then I slipped into a pair of ankle-laced, low-heeled sandals.

I considered replacing my clear nail varnish with red. But the thought of having to apply nail varnish remover to each toe put me off the idea

If I fussed around any more, I'd be late for my rendezvous with Afet. I had to leave immediately. I called the taxi stand. I was certain Hüseyin, who's practically my private chauffeur, would be the one to pick me up. And he was.

"*Merhaba*," he greets me.

He paused, arm draped over the seat, turning back to give me a long look. Everyone at the stand knows this is around the time I go to the club. So had Hüseyin.

"What are you waiting for," I asked. "Let's get going."

"You don't give me so much as the time of day anymore."

I'm not sure how I look at him. But he instantly turned round.

"I'm not in a very good mood tonight," I apologised. "Forgive me."

He continued talking, as though to himself.

"Some people can make others feel better. But they're never given a chance."

He was flirting with me again. Persistent as ever. What's

more, he knows I resent being addressed by the familiar "*sen*", rather than the formal "*siz*". He was deliberately switching from one to the other.

Hüseyin never misses an opportunity to proclaim his passion for me. No matter how strongly I object, he persists, never losing hope. He follows me whenever possible, a bit like an unwanted shadow. When he isn't giving me reproachful glances, though, he does manage to keep the car on the road.

I have told him dozens of times that he just isn't my type. But one day, in a moment of weakness, at a time when I needed love and affection, he had enjoyed my favours. That was it. He's been after me ever since. I don't like, nor am I capable of liking, men who beg. I prefer men with a sense of pride. Not clingers. If he really wants me, he'll grab me by the arm, drag me off and take me. Of course, cultivating this air of helplessness is part of the act. And part of the fun. No one who really knows me would dare. Everyone in the neighbourhood is aware of my skills in Aikido and Thai boxing. As is Hüseyin. Perhaps he's just biding his time.

Three

Cüneyt, the club bouncer, greeted me at the door. It was still early. He had nothing better to do than hold the door open for those arriving and leaving. But I'm special. After all, I am the boss, even if my stake in the club is a small one. And I am totally in charge.

As I got out of the taxi, Hüseyin, true to form, proposed returning to pick me up. Not straying from our well-established routine, I refused him.

"Boss," observed Cüneyt, as he held open the door for me, "you sure treat that guy bad."

I flashed upon him the look of contempt he so richly deserved.

"But then again," he corrected himself, "who am I to ..."

"Exactly," I snapped. Short and sweet.

Particularly when it comes to my employees, I have rather limited tolerance for presumptuous behaviour. That is, none. No one could expect anything different. That said, I do have a certain amount of sympathy for Cüneyt. If nothing else, the boy is just so comical. He makes me laugh. Then there is his showy body, a critical attribute for a club doorman and the result of nearly daily sessions at the gym. He is also so refreshingly simple. By that, I do not refer to his intelligence, but to his purity. His naivety, if you will. Cüneyt just has a different way of looking at things, a degree of empathy that even I find excessive. Most importantly, he approaches his job with the utmost seriousness.

The club was empty. DJ Osman, barman Şükrü and our waiter, Hasan, were huddled together talking. When they saw me, they sprang to attention.

"Is everything all right, boss?" asked Şükrü. "You're early tonight."

"I have an appointment. With Afet," I answered.

"I'll get your Virgin Mary immediately," said Şükrü. It is my habit to have my drink ready and handed to me the moment I enter the club. Then again, there was no way he could have known that I would arrive early.

Taking advantage of the absence of customers – or rather, my absence – Osman was playing his favourite ear-splitting heavy metal. With the club empty, and the lack of a general din to absorb the thudding, the music was even more violently audible than usual.

Taking his cue from my severe expression, Osman rushed to the DJ booth to change the music.

I wa left alone with Hasan.

"*Merhaba*," he greeted me. "Did you find out anything?"

"Not really," I admitted. "It's clear she didn't die in that house. I smell a rat. I'm afraid the girl suffered."

"I got to thinking after I talked to you... You're right. There's definitely something funny going on here."

"The police won't bother to look into it. They've already closed her file."

"You're right," he agreed. "But there are still municipality and fire department investigations."

It was now my turn to agree.

We looked at each other for a moment in silence. Osman had changed the music to some kind of elevator muzak. He returned, fighting off a smirk. In the middle of the table, a glass of mandarin soda, over half full, awaited him. No one else in the club drinks mandarin soda. None of the customers have ever ordered one. But it is the only thing he touches. Two cases a month are brought in for his personal use.

"What's this music you're playing?" I demanded.

"Adiemus. New Age. It's a new group. Great isn't it?"

To add insult to injury, he was poking fun at me. New Age is one of the forms of music I simply don't comprehend. Paul Mauriat, Franck Pourcel, Francis Lai and even Fausto Papetti have been playing this kind of music for years. The only difference is that they perform with an orchestra, not synthesisers and the piping of a flute. Nowadays, intellectuals have elevated this sort of music into an art form. Why the double standard? What have the others been doing wrong all these years? A succession of critics has slammed them. All right, I don't think much of their work either, but I don't see the difference. Do you?

"Look here!" I snapped. "Don't push me. Go put on something decent!"

"Right, boss," he said, straight back to the DJ booth.

Once again, Hasan and I were tête-à-tête.

"I tried to reach Gül. But I failed."

Hasan spoke of failure, but he is in fact extremely gifted. What's more, he's sharp as a pin. He also loves gossip; he makes a point of inspiring and encouraging it. And he's shameless about spreading stories. If there's nothing to repeat, he just makes something up. There's something crafty about everything he does. He thirsts for treachery and duplicity. He's also the number one accomplice of Sofya, the patron saint of such matters.

Halfway to the booth, Osman turned to shout: "Turkish or foreign?"

"Turkish! But no wailing. And nothing too fast."

I wouldn't put it past him to go and play Mahsun Kırmızıgül, a Kurdish *arabesque* singer who wails along to a disco beat and goes by the stage name "Sad Red Rose". Then I'd have an excuse to give him a good thrashing. In any case, I have been looking for a way to let off some steam.

"As you know, Ceren's been hanging out with Gül lately," Hasan continued.

"I learned that from you."

My Virgin Mary arrived. There were still no customers, so Şükrü joined us at the table.

"No one knows where Gül is," observed Hasan, adding, "Şükrü sweetie, could you get me a soda with ice?"

"Why didn't you ask when I was at the bar? I just got here."

"Sorry about that. I forgot."

You'd have to be a fool not to realise that Hasan was doing this on purpose. The kids at the club tell me any number of stories about how he promotes himself to manager in my absence and give them all a hard time. But then again, he can be so appealing. It's difficult to get cross with Hasan. He has a lovable quality, "a hair of the devil" as the saying goes, and is on intimate terms instantly with everyone. That is, he is nothing like me. Although he hasn't allowed Şükrü to sit for even a moment, there will be no grudges. It is still to Hasan that Şükrü will first reveal his secrets. Naturally, Hasan will then come and repeat them to me.

"Who is this Gül?" I asked.

"She's new," Hasan answered. "Very young. A pink and white thing."

Şükrü returned with an iced lemon soda, and jumped into the conversation.

"I saw her once. She was a real piece of Turkish delight. Something to nibble on. You get the picture." Even Şükrü has shining eyes as he describes her. "But I kept my distance. She was jailbait."

"What do you mean?" I quizzed him.

"She was sixteen at most," explained Hasan. "She came here twice, but we didn't let her in."

"She didn't even have a beard yet," Şükrü pointed out.

They know my unbending rule. No customers under eighteen years of age. I loathe complications. I don't want the police on our backs for something as silly as that. There are clubs that let them in, that serve them drinks. But my club is not, and will never be, one of those establishments.

The door opens, and Cüneyt showed in Afet. Her hair was gathered into a tight bun. As a result, the angular lines of her face were even more strained than usual. Clearly, she had spent at least an hour applying eye makeup. Less than half a metre of cloth had been used to clothe her in a creation that passed for a dress, and sequins were liberally applied all across her throat and breasts. Afet totters precariously on that thin line dividing the ridiculously strange from the strangely beautiful. Her feet are large, even for a transvestite. Even so, she had chosen to emphasise them, spilling out of tiny high-heels. As usual, knees slightly bent, she appeared poised to leap forward.

While it was quite a show, it is far from my idea of true elegance.

As the proprietor, I rose to greet her. We exchanged air kisses.

"Don't ask! I found out after you phoned. Ceren is dead, *abla*," she began. "I'm simply shattered."

We settled at a table away from the boys. Hasan immediately came up to ask what we'd like to drink.

"Whisky," she said. "No ice. You have got Johnny Walker?"

"Of course," said Hasan, indignant.

"One of those, then." She turned to me and continued. "They said a fire broke out at her flat. I was terrified. We live in the same building, you know. Then I realised I was being ridiculous. I mean, I'd surely notice a fire in my own apartment. Wouldn't I, *abla*?"

I do not enjoy being referred to as "*abla*". Not one bit. But now was not the time for a warning. First, I'd learn all I could, then I'd put her in her place. For now, I settled for a smile.

The whisky arrived. She beamed her thanks. Screwing up her face, she took her first sip.

"Ohhh . . . That does the trick,"

I didn't ask her the reason for the facial contortions.

"So you found out about it," I said. "She died in an abandoned building in Tarlabaşı."

Afet leapt on the information. "What on earth was she doing there? Of course, it's true she had a total disregard for danger. And all she cared about was putting aside some money. She was determined to have the operation, as you know. Then she said she would get a house, a car and a handsome, young husband. But sweetie, there is just no way anyone would go off with a bunch of strange men to some forsaken spot on Tarlabaşı! Well tell me. Is there?"

"You're right."

"I know I shouldn't say this, but she really had it coming."

I froze. As did she, realising what she'd just said.

"That's not what I meant. It's just that I'm still so cross with her." She motioned with her eyes to Hasan. "He told you about it?"

He had, of course. But I played dumb.

"I don't remember."

"It was the most unbelievable thing! Quite astonishing, really. I can understand it happening once or twice, my dear, but not all the time. She'd be at my door asking to borrow whatever she'd seen me wearing two days earlier. I'd give her what she wanted, telling myself she was young, new, and eager to model herself on others. But there was no returning anything. What she took was as good as gone. Now if she had just appreciated their value. I'm not at all selfish. You know that."

Nearby, the trio of Hasan, Şükrü and Osman were eavesdropping on us. Not a peep came from their table.

"I'm afraid I blew my top one morning while I was hanging out the laundry. I saw her in a tunic I'd paid Belkis a small fortune for. Darling, I mean, it's not her wearing it . . . but while washing the balcony? There's such a thing as being a little too decadent. And I work hard for every penny."

"You're right," I assured her, with a smile of commiseration.

"To tell the truth, she was the very picture of bad manners. Whenever she wanted something, it was 'darling Afet' this, 'sweetie Afet' that. Other times, she wouldn't give me the time of day. I just won't stand for that sort of thing."

I didn't ask the reason for her falling out with Fatoş *abla*.

The door opened and the first group of girls flitted in. While it would not seem humanly possible for four girls to make such a racket, succeed they did. We exchanged greetings.

"One day, on the staircase, she tried to hustle someone who'd just left my place. That was the last straw."

To be honest, that sort of behaviour makes me cross, too. But I still didn't believe she deserved to die.

"*Abla*, what do you think will happen to her flat?" So, she had recovered from her grief and was now focused on the flat below hers. "The police won't seal it off, will they?"

"I don't think so," I assured her.

"Good. I've been working at home lately. I have a few regulars. You understand. The last thing I need is trouble with the police."

I did understand.

Another group of girls came in, immediately followed by two men dressed like fruit vendors. While I'm not attracted to that particular type, I do appreciate their patronage. They hold their liquor like gentlemen, treat the girls to drinks and plates of sliced fruit, and leave big tips, as a way of showing off. In short, they're big spenders. They don't make trouble, and leave with whichever girl they fancy.

I recognised one of them, and nodded a greeting. He responded, with reverence.

The boys were back to manning their stations. Two young neighbourhood toughs had also arrived, and were checking out the club with looks of hunger and insolence. They chose a spot far from the dance floor, against the wall but with a good view. The girls began getting in gear. Naturally, most of them prefer young men. Even if they don't earn as much money, off they go, saying they are "doing it for fun".

Customers come early for one of two reasons: To make a selection while there are still plenty of girls or to return home at a reasonable hour. But there's a drawback, which is a bit of common knowledge: The girls are more expensive early at night. As dawn approaches, the price of the unchosen falls.

And the club sprang to life.

Four

Time flies when it's crowded, and sometimes I don't even realise morning has come. When Osman plays my favourite songs – and he knows perfectly well what would happen if he didn't – I rise and dance. I never dance to two songs back to back. I would perspire. My appearance would be compromised. It is my custom to dance for just one song at a time.

While they may not be the latest thing, the Weather Girls' "It's Raining Men", Eartha Kitt's "Where is My Man" and the first version of Ajda Pekkan's "Uykusuz Her Gece (Sleepless Every Night)", along with, sometimes, "Bambaşka Biri (Someone Completely Different)", are definitely played in my honour, as well as a Grace Jones or RuPaul number. I'm also fond of many of today's hits, giving me another excuse to dance.

The girls, for their part, use the dance floor to display their charms to potential customers. Anyone wanting some attention simply heads for the dance floor and lets rip. If they get along well with Osman, he'll arrange a spotlight. And the show begins.

If Osman has a bone to pick, though, he'll cut a tune right off, or speed up or slow it down. In other words, he'll most definitely find a way to ruin the show. If nothing else, the spot disappears and the eager performer is left in the dark.

I have one unbending rule: girls are not to strip on stage. If one dares to, off go the lights. The girl guilty of exposing this or that bit of flesh is issued a warning. Those who persist are barred from the premises. Everyone is absolutely familiar with this rule.

Those desperate to show off their wares are free to do so at the tables in the back; to this, I have no objections. Provided they maintain a sense of discretion, the girls are allowed to promote themselves. Some of the more self-confident young men, that is, those who take pride in their bodies, also make an appearance on the dance floor. Once again, I have no objections. I countenance anything aesthetically pleasing, and even enjoy watching.

As for the occasional flaunting of underdeveloped musculatures, I leave it to Osman to handle things.

Furthermore, I expect male patrons, as well, to proceed to the shadowy tables at the back. Nothing is to be done out in the open!

Ahmet Kuyu, an actor well past his prime, arrived some time later. For us, his claim to fame has more to do with his infamously poor treatment of our girls than his old films. To date, not a single one of the girls who has escorted him from the club has escaped without a bruised face. I have been fully briefed on his other nasty and shameless tricks. Despite having been taken to an inner room and given a warning, he has dared to come again. Cüneyt must not have noticed, since Ahmet has come as part of a large group.

They were also a mixed group, in terms of age, attire and of course economic status. In view of Ahmet Kuyu's smarmy deference, the most important person in the group was a man who could be considered fairly young. He was looking around with an air of superior interest. His clothing was smart, but casual. Not a style I admire. His face seemed familiar, but I couldn't place it. He is probably a TV producer, someone able to land a long-awaited role for Ahmet Kuyu. Our sadistic actor has not appeared in a film for years, and is rarely given a role, even in one of those disagreeable series shown on dozens of channels.

There were no ladies. Large groups such as this one tend to drag along a couple of curious women, who are inevitably the most enthusiastic of the bunch. Some wish to check out what they consider the competition. Once they do, their worlds collapse. Our girls, at least the majority of them, are so very superior. With their sense of flair, airs, manners, make-up and movements, our girls are just so much more feminine. More attractive. More . . . titillating.

The disappointed woman in question resorts to humour. It's the best way to deal. Realising it's difficult – even impossible – to compete, the whole thing must be presented as a farce. They laugh incessantly. They imagine they are making fun of the girls. But they cannot avoid one simple fact. Perhaps not this particular night, but most certainly some time in the future, the men accompanying them will slip out of their hands and into bed with one of our girls.

This knowledge damns them. As the cost of satisfying their curiosity, it is absolutely appropriate. They will never fully recover.

Ahmet Kuyu's group ordered some pricey drinks. I gestured Hasan over to ask who the mystery man was. Hasan knows everyone and everything.

"Adem Yıldız," he promptly informed me. "Heir to the Yıldız supermarket chain."

The moment I heard the name I remembered having come across his photographs in business magazines. That's right, the father transformed a patisserie in a third-rate neighbourhood into a chain of supermarkets spreading across Turkey. And Adem Yıldız is his son. As far as I recalled, they were a conservative group of companies, rumoured to be in with the *hacı-hoca* lot. This isn't public knowledge. In order to avoid carrying alcohol, they run their stores not as normal supermarkets, but as expanded patisseries. They even export a whole range of their own products, from biscuits and ice cream, to *börek* and *lokum*.

A steady stream of girls sat at, and then rose from, their tables. Each one was treated to a drink. Ahmet Kuyu assumed the role of go-between. He would rise, call a girl over, introduce her to Ahmet Yıldız and then sit grinning stupidly in response to one of his own jokes. Then the process was repeated. The traffic was exhausting. Needing a break, I looked away.

I suddenly remembered that regulars in the chat room have assumed nicks like "adam-star", "starman" and "*adam". Adem Yıldız. Adem, the Turkish for "Adam" or "man", and Yıldız, a word for "star". Any of the nicks could have been inspired by this name. I tried to remember what the various authors had written in the chat room, but nothing sprang to mind. There couldn't have been anything memorable. Or I would most certainly have recalled it. Could this Adem Yıldız be one of the chat room regulars?

I didn't appreciate the way Adem was looking at the girls. A mixture of loathing and desire was registered on his face. I supposed it was natural for someone raised by such a conservative family. But I still found it hard to believe that this was his first encounter with a live transvestite.

That's right, coming to see a "live" transvestite, like coming to enjoy "live" music. I dislike those who visit the club for that reason. However, this is a commercial establishment, and we do have to chase after our daily bread.

Of the girls I had spoken to, all were familiar with Gül's legendary beauty. But they had different opinions about how she could be reached; her reputed haunts range from the beer houses of Aksaray to the streets of Harbiye.

Sırma, blunt as they come, put her finger on it. "I wish that girl would hit the jackpot; then the rest of us would get a turn at the trough." I was obviously the only person not well-acquainted with Gül, who was viewed by the others mainly as a formidable rival.

In the middle of my back, on my bare skin, I felt the sudden touch of a rough, hot hand. I do not appreciate being fondled at will. I spun around to see Ali, with an attractive man at his side.

Grasping and fairly young, Ali owns the computer consulting company that employs me. While ignorant of computer systems, he is a real genius when it comes to sales and marketing. We'd worked together on any number of projects, with the result that he had earned a small fortune. Generally, we are hired to protect major companies, including international ones, from computer viruses. As hackers proliferate, and new viruses are spread through e-mail, we enjoy burgeoning business opportunities. Otherwise, we make a modest living from designing websites and handling standard updates.

I'm not accustomed to seeing Ali in the club. I was astonished. At our meetings, I am always dressed in a far more manly fashion. It wasn't as though he hadn't seen me like this though; he had even stopped by the club before. But I still felt strange.

"*Merhaba*," he greeted me. "You look fabulous."

He is not a convincing liar. I looked terrible. I'd attempted to pull off an outdated, amusing look. And had succeeded. So why did he insist on treating me like a vamp?

"Let me introduce you," he continued. "This is my squash partner, Cengiz."

"Pleased to meet you," I said.

Cengiz held my hand for a long moment. It was a definite signal. He was handsome, and not as young as I had thought at first glance. Definitely past forty, even somewhere in his late forties. But with his tanned face and sparkling, deep eyes, his charisma was fully intact.

"Ali talked about you so much I wanted a chance to meet," he explained.

"What did he say?"

Ali immediately jumped in.

"You know how I sing your praises."

"My skills, my expertise when it comes to computers. Yes. But I wasn't aware of your tributes to my present condition."

"I insisted we come," said Cengiz. "Won't you have a drink with us? I'd like to get to know you better."

He was openly flirting. It had been a matter of just a few seconds since he laid eyes on me. Why had he chosen me from among all the girls?

"I don't drink alcohol at the club," I demurred.

"Have something else, then," he insisted.

Ali was grinning as he watched us. He's the last person I'd have expected to assume the role of matchmaker, but that certainly seemed to be the case.

I dispensed with coquetry, and we moved to a table. Ali droned on about irrelevant and insignificant business details. Clearly, he'd had too much to drink. Normally, he wasn't that talkative.

From our table, I had a clear view of Adem Yıldız and Ahmet Kuyu. I couldn't help glancing over. Elvan was sitting with them. Ahmet was fondling and grabbing at the girls he had brought to the table. Adem just watched. It would be more accurate to say that he looked on hungrily. I couldn't begin to fathom the way his mind was weighing things up, the calculations that were going through his head.

Meanwhile, Cengiz was at my table and a fine-looking man indeed. All his attention was focused on me, and he didn't even steal glances at the dance floor.

"I like your club. It's got an ambience all its own."

What he meant, of course, is that it is a tolerable dive. Others have said the same

"Isn't that Adem Yıldız and Ahmet Kuyu sitting over there?" asked Ali.

Ali keeps up on the business world, regarding anyone with money as a potential partner, a customer. Certainly, he would know Adem Yıldız. His familiarity with Ahmet Kuyu surprised me, though. The man's star faded and burned out years ago. The fifth-rate TV series he occasionally appears in aren't shown at times when Ali would be watching.

"That's right," I said. "It's them."

"Wow," Ali exclaimed. "You get all sorts here . . . "

"The Yıldız family has a place next to my summer house,"

said Cengiz. "I didn't notice him when we arrived."

"*Abi*, how about a plate of flaming fruit?" suggested Ali, proving he is smashed.

We all burst out laughing, and Cengiz seized the chance to throw an arm around my shoulder and draw me to him.

Five

Those days my heart was empty, but my arms were full most nights. I must have been going through a horny phase. I'd been sleeping with a series of strange men. I can always tell the arrival of autumn by the increase in my libido. I've been that way for years.

The balmy, humid nature of summer nights in Istanbul makes it difficult to tolerate a warm body in bed – even my own. I toss and turn from side to side, sleeping slanted across the sheets if have to. Then, when my own body heat has made one side unbearable, I move to the relative cool of the other. That's how I spend my summer nights.

But with the turning of the season and the autumn cool, especially before the central heating comes on, it's nice to sleep with a man in my arms. It warms me. I hold him; he embraces me. We sleep that way, all toasty.

I opened my eyes in the first light of dawn. My bedroom curtains are thick, barring all light. There's no way to know that morning has come, when in my bedroom. But if the door is open, sunlight streams in from the spacious living room windows, fills the corridor and trickles into my room. Beams of light play across the floors. What I describe here is my house. But I was not now in my bedroom. The thin curtains were allowing the sun to fill the room in which I had been lying all morning long.

I looked at the man in my arms. Well, not exactly in my arms. His back was turned, and he'd claimed most of the covers. I'd been sleeping half uncovered, which may be the reason I woke up.

I tried to tug the covers towards me. But failed. He was wrapped tightly in them. One foot poked out below. I don't have a fetish, but I must give the foot its due. It was a superb and shapely specimen.

I snuggled closer in an attempt to get warm. As I got nearer, he let out a snort and moved towards the edge of the bed. Egoist. There'd be a reckoning when he rose.

I had to pee. I must have caught a chill, or I wouldn't normally get up this early to go to the bathroom. I used the toilet, then looked at myself in the mirror. Traces of makeup covered an unshaven face. My short hair was mussed and my puffy eyes not the least bit attractive.

As I always say, I am a perfect example of the wonders of makeup. While I'm quite handsome as a man, well-applied makeup transforms me into a goddess of the silver screen. Not the stars of this day and age. I refer to the glitteringly glamorous Hollywood stars of the '50s and '60s.

A shaving kit lay ready before the mirror. But I had no desire to use it. He knew what he went to bed with. My current state should not surprise him. Furthermore, he kept a firm grip on it all night long. Or at least until he fell asleep and turned his back.

Once I get out of bed, there's no returning. So I washed my face, and applied styling gel to what had degenerated into a post-punk hairdo. A courteous-looking young man then gazed at me from the looking glass. I had become me.

The morning chill licked at my skin, and I got goose bumps. I considered getting dressed, but changed my mind. There's nothing like wandering nude in homes not one's own, especially when they belong to rich men like the cover stealer.

I inspected the kitchen, with the intention of preparing breakfast. Every kind of tea imaginable was on offer, but no coffee. Apparently, some people do not drink the stuff. Rows of vitamins, natural juices and oatmeal highlighted his obvious attention to his health, also illustrated by his flat stomach.

Pictures of children were fastened with magnets to the fridge. Two boys, both with his thick head of hair. They were fairer than their father. Or it could be that age has darkened his hair, and tennis and the solarium his skin. It was difficult to guess the ages of the boys, but it would be at least another ten years, maybe even a dozen, before they would be of any use. What's more, I prefer mature sorts, like their father.

I rummaged through the fridge while waiting for the kettle to boil. Like most bachelors, his was empty except for a couple of bottles of white wine, milk, eggs, types of cheese and a variety of exotic sausages. Also, bottles of health tonics and energy drinks. I examined the label of one of them. If the bottle really contained what it claimed to, I would become still hornier after drinking its contents. I put it back. The water was now boiling in any case.

I put a lemon teabag into a cobalt blue mug with gilded edges. I didn't fill it to the brim with hot water, removing the tea bag and adding room temperature water so I could drink it right away.

The newspapers had arrived. I took my tea and the papers into the living room. It had an amazing view of the Bosphorus.

Lit up from behind, the Asian shore seemed almost ghostly. It was a crisp, bright day. The sun streams in. Putting aside the paper, I decided to enjoy the scenery, the beauty of which I had failed to appreciate fully the previous night.

Before me lay a bird's eye view of the Bosphorus from the hills of Ulus. Ships were gliding through the dark blue sea. A grove of pines stood between the house and the water. A brilliant emerald. I recalled how much of Istanbul's greenery has disappeared, and sighed. My grandmother's claim that "Istanbul didn't use to be half this green; the hilltops along the Bosphorus were totally bare," didn't stop me from indulging in a false nostalgia for "green Istanbul".

Captivated by the view, I sipped my tea. It was still far too early for me to hit the street. And he didn't seem to have any intention of waking up just yet. My stomach grumbled, but I was certainly going nowhere near that oatmeal. A fruit bowl contained two peaches. I ate them both.

Then I made another tea. I settled into the same deep leather chair. As the morning light changes, watching the Bosphorus is like viewing a film. The opposite shore was now illuminated in a completely differently way. Each and every moment had a visual drama all its own.

From somewhere inside I could hear the sound of a toilet flushing, followed by gargling. So Cengiz had got out of bed. I shifted into a more alluring pose. He was soon at my side. Also naked. As always with those proud of their bodies.

He was smiling.

"You're up early," he remarked.

He leaned down to kiss me, his breath smelling of mint mouthwash.

Sitting down in the armchair opposite, he began scrutinising me. His eyes were still bleary with sleep; I couldn't tell what he was looking at, or how it affected him.

"You're quite something like this too."

I knew it. I know men like Cengiz. He was intending to go at it again. I simply smiled.

He rose, came to my side and kissed me again. He was full of desire. But I was not. I stood up and slipped free.

"The kettle's boiled. I'll go make you a cup of tea."

Cengiz moved into my chair as I headed for the kitchen.

When I brought in his tea he thanked me. He was looking at the newspaper. His morning passion had subsided.

"Another transvestite's dead. Have you seen this?" he asked.

"It was in the paper yesterday. A fire," I answered.

"No, not that," he said. "Another one. Drowned in a cistern. Have you seen it?"

I hadn't. The paper had been there all morning, but I hadn't even scanned the headlines. So much for relegating transvestite deaths to the third page.

A dead transvestite a day. It was truly upsetting. Yesterday Ceren, and then today... Gül! Even in the regulation snapshot she was breathtakingly beautiful. And, according to the paper, all of seventeen.

Gül was found dead in a well in Kücükyalı. It is no longer used because of the new coastal road. The cause of death was drowning. The coroner's office is investigating.

I must have looked as distraught as I felt. Cengiz perched on the arm of my chair. He stroked my shoulder without a word. At first, I was annoyed; then I felt comforted.

Six

Could it all be a coincidence? First Ceren, and then young Gül, her hooking partner, were found dead. It didn't seem at all normal to me.

One died in Tarlabasi, far from her home, in a fire in an abandoned building. The other drowned in a well belonging to an unused house, on the Asian shore of Istanbul, in Kücükyalı, a neighbourhood not particularly fruitful for transvestites. The two girls were friends. While it's true that genuine friendships are the exception among us, they did at least have an intimate working relationship. Perhaps Gül, so new to the scene, hoped to build herself a new life by working with the more experienced Ceren.

When I get home I begin surfing newspapers on the internet for more information. Nothing I found seemed significant.

Gül's real name was Yusuf Seçkin. She was from the Black Sea. So Şükrü must have been referring to her general complexion when he described her as "pink and white".

It was particularly noteworthy that she became a transvestite while still a mere child. Morals and national values are apparently in jeopardy. I decided, as soon as possible, to crash the website claiming this. This sort of thing doesn't happen through mere imitation, or because of a so-called role model.

There was no news of the child-transvestite's family.

Abandoned wells are a grave public threat. What is the municipality doing? Measures must be taken. The reporter and editor responsible for drawing such lessons from the death deserved a good thrashing.

Next, I of course rang Hasan.

"Şükrü fell apart when he heard the news. I've been trying to comfort him," he said. "You know he was such a fan."

"What do you know?" I demanded.

"Nothing at the moment. If I find out anything I'll let you know," he assured me.

I showered at Cengiz's, but he'd been unable to keep his hands off me, and I felt sticky. I took a quick shower and got ready to go out. It's best to go to the morgue looking like a real gentleman. They would have the most detailed account of the deaths.

A small bribe and a smile should get me the information I needed. I managed to reach the doctor on duty after getting past her insubordinates. She was a particularly ugly woman, and I hesitated on whether or not to pay her a compliment on her appearance.

I decided to be merely gracious. I explained my problem in moving tones. I appealed to her conscience. While I doubted that such a thin, dried-up vessel could possibly harbour any-thing resembling a conscience, I suppressed that thought.

She watched me intently, without speaking.

"And are you one of them?" she asked.

I despise such questions, which I find them overly aggressive. I don't claim to "pass". But, given my general condition, outfit and two-day stubble, I was a bit shaken by being asked so directly.

Madame doctor smiled at me knowingly.

"It doesn't matter," she said. "Some of my best friends are gay. I have no problem with it."

If she expected her indulgence to be rewarded with gratitude, she was sadly mistaken. I detected a hint of malice in her words. My reserves of tolerance are limited. I felt myself getting annoyed.

"Are you going to help me?" I asked.

"We'll see."

She did not say what we would see or even what she expected from me. The words "hideous bitch" passed through my mind.

She was still giving me the once over. I responded by doing the same. Actually, the general contours of her face were not entirely objectionable, and each of her appendages, when viewed independently, was more or less normal. But the sum of her parts was a repulsive sight indeed. Her badly dyed hair had become the colour of flesh, and over-enthusiastic applications of hairspray had produced an impenetrable helmet. Apart from being merely puffy, it had no style what so ever. She looked like a schoolmistress who stands ready, ruler in hand, to pounce on the first schoolboy to giggle.

There was no wedding ring, which was unsurprising. Her eyebrows had been plucked nearly to extinction, and were thin, arched and shaped like parentheses. They contributed to the general tension of her face. Her makeup was virtually non-existent, but managed to be disastrous none the less.

She pursed her lips as she stared.

"I'm doing some research," she revealed.

I knew full well and immediately that any such research would result in no good. But I kept my mouth shut.

"On homosexuals," she elaborated.

"So?" I prompted her.

"I would like you to participate."

I was unable to resist asking the nature of her research. I had every right to learn what I faced and whether or not it was worth the information I sought.

She aggressively twirled her pen. Obviously she was weighing her words, wondering how to get an affirmative response out of me.

"Our research focuses primarily on vice cases and homosexuals who have applied for treatment to the venereal clinic."

I was astonished. Apparently, some of the girls check into the clinic of their own accord. I'd been under the impression that they were ushered to the hospital after being rounded up during police raids. The girls choose only the best doctors and private hospitals. Being sent to the venereal clinic is more of a punitive measure, like going to jail.

"The research is of a practical nature and concerns changes and deformation exhibited by the sphincter."

I wondered if I'd heard her right.

"Meaning?"

I didn't care if she found me ignorant. I needed to know her exact intentions concerning my bottom.

"Basic measurements," she explained. "We measure alterations in the constriction of the sphincter. As well as deformation exhibited by the rectum and surrounding areas."

"I think I understand," I gently murmured.

"Oh. And there's also a brief survey," she added. "Questions concerning your past sexual history, experiences, frequency of intercourse and so forth. Naturally, you are not required to use your real name."

"I'm happy to fill out a survey, but I have no intention of revealing my rectal details."

She was astonished by my reluctance.

"We won't hurt you. It may smart just a bit."

"That's not the problem. It's just the idea of a metal instrument entering my bum."

What was the name of that instrument? Something like a gyroscope or a periscope. I got annoyed at not being able to remember.

"Rectoscopy," she informed me.

"No thank you."

"You know best," she said, leaning towards the papers in front of her.

When she saw I remained in the chair, she fixed her eyes on me, without raising her head.

"And now if you'll excuse me, I've got work to do."

Yuck! She'd obviously grown up with Turkish films of the '60s. What kind of line was that?

She had no intention of helping me. Until she had measured my sphincter, conducted a rectoscopy, handled and investigated my arse, she would reveal nothing concerning Ceren and Gül. That much was clear.

Actually, there was no need for her to tell me anything. Letting me glance through the files would be enough. She looked at me like a teacher's pet about to tattle.

I got up.

Seven

I ran into Gönül at the door of the forensic department. This, the most ignorant and impudent member of our little circle, tends to make an appearance either at the forensic department or at funerals.

As always, she was in tears. She was wearing a loose print skirt covered with a busy pattern and held up, I suspected, by an elastic waist band. Hanging down to the ground, it was teamed with a white T-shirt emblazoned with a peacock design in sequins. Spotting me, she paused and fixed me with a long, hard look.

"You owe me a meal."

It was not quite what one would expect as an opening line, particularly from somebody so histrionically weeping.

"A promise is a promise," I assured her.

"But I've lost your phone number. How do I find you?"

I gave her my number again. The one at the office, where it's most difficult to reach me. I go there once a week at most, but the secretary takes messages.

Her grief implied that she was bosom buddies with Ceren and Gül. I asked for confirmation.

"What have I to do with Ceren? She was real scum. Yusuf is another story. I'm crying for him."

She resumed sobbing.

"I brought him here from Rize. He was a blonde Laz boy, all pink and white, with hair like corn silk. He was just like a girl. And wanted so badly to be one. I took him along with me for company. But then that whore Ceren separated us."

I was on the scent. Gönül bursts into tears again. It was going to be impossible to get any more information out of her here. If I got her on her own, though, who knows what she would tell me.

"What do you say to a bite to eat now?" I suggested.

A smile slowly crept across her face, a face now nearly devoid of makeup. She was determined to get that promised meal. Gönül pointed to the forensic building.

"Let me just find out what's going on," she said.

"I'll wait," I told her.

"Promise?"

I promised. And confirmed it with a wink. She responded with a flirtatious kiss, then disappeared into the dreary forensic building.

I waited for nearly half an hour. She finally appeared, muttering to herself.

"I told them I was her guardian. What nasty people! No help at all. Anyway, there was this lady doctor. A pitiful, pig-headed thing. She's doing some kind of study; she told me to come tomorrow morning on an empty stomach."

Gönül told me all this in a single breath. Then inhaled deeply. I was certain she had no idea what awaited her the next day. There was no need to sabotage myself by telling her about the rectoscopy. I held my tongue.

"Where are we going?" she asked.

"Wherever you like."

"Would you go to Beyoğlu?"

"Of course."

"So you won't be embarrassed to be seen with me?"

"Of course not. Don't be stupid," I reassured her.

"If you'd rather not, just tell me. I don't mind. Some people would rather not be seen with me."

She had a strange habit of swallowing her 'r's. I hadn't noticed it before. Perhaps she believed it gave her an air of refinement.

"What do you mean," I protested. I took her arm and steered her towards the taxi rank.

The moment we sat down, I gave in to my curiosity.

"Tell me everything," I demanded.

"Not in the taxi," she refused. "I'll tell you at the restaurant."

Something had happened to the nightingale of a few moments earlier. She'd got it into her head to be bashful in front of the taxi driver.

"Why don't we get out in Tünel or Galatasaray? Then we can walk to Taksim," she suggested.

"Where would you like to eat?" I asked.

"You decide. I chose the area; you choose the restaurant. You're paying; it's up to you."

I racked my brain, trying to think of an out-of-the-way place where we could speak openly and not be harassed by anyone. I came up empty.

True to form, Gönül began flirting with the driver. We all have our peculiarities. From what I've heard, the mere sight of a hand gripping a steering wheel is enough to seduce Gönül. Type and age are minor details to be dealt with later.

"Brother, where are you from?" she began.

Our driver was from Iğdır.

When Gönül heard the word "Iğdır" she inhaled so deeply you'd think she was sniffing at the elixir of eternal youth. The driver turned around with an alarmed expression.

"You really know how to handle a car," she continued.

I felt a slow flush creeping up to my forehead. The driver began watching us in his rear-view mirror. There was no mistaking who and what we were, but he seemed uncertain how to respond.

We crossed Unkapani Bridge and were approaching the cross-roads in Kasımpaşa. The driver asked the standard question.

"Galatasaray or Tünel? Which'll it be?

Gönül seized the chance to get him involved.

"Which do you think would be better?" she fluted.

I was sure Gönül was kicking herself for not sitting in front.

"I mean, we're grabbing a bite to eat. Is there a place you'd recommend? Maybe you know somewhere nice?"

I looked out of the window to conceal my embarrassment. The dark driver was staring at me in the mirror. I flushed even deeper.

"You're welcome to come with us." Gönül suddenly turned to me. "That'd be all right, huh? For my sake, *abla*?"

On top of everything else, referring to me, while dressed as a man, as "big sister"! I didn't know what to do. Why on earth would the taxi driver come to eat with us? He hadn't said a word, just looked at us in the mirror. Because we didn't give him directions, he opted to turn into Tünel, and was now heading for Galatasaray.

"I'm just wild about Eastern men."

Everything Gönül says, no matter what it is, verges on the obscene. And her facial expressions are fit only for porn.

"In fact, I'm from the East myself. From Van." She was

clearly flirting, while licking her lips non-stop like some actress in a German sex flick.

"There's nothing like the men out East."

The driver turned out to be a real gentleman. He turned into Tepebaşı, and then stopped at Odakule.

He pointed to a building next to Odakule, not even looking at us.

"The top floor of that building."

I quickly handed over the fare, then tried to open the left-hand door. The sooner I got out in the street the better. The door refused to open.

"It's broken. You'll have to use the other side," he said.

Gönül opened her door, but had no intention of getting out.

"What if we can't find it? Come on, why don't you escort us?"

He pointed to the building once again.

"The top floor," he said. "It's called Mefharet, or Meserret or something like that."

He gave me my change and I gave Gönül a push. She had to be shoved.

"He was such a looker! Just my type," she sighed. "And you didn't help out one bit. Shame on you!"

I grinned foolishly, the last resort of the truly speechless. It can signal understanding, humility or apology. I left the interpretation to Gönül.

We took the lift to the top floor, then climbed a flight of stairs to a rooftop terrace with a sweeping view of the Golden Horn. The waterfront districts of Balat, Fener and Ayvansaray lay before us. There aren't many customers, which was a good thing.

I wanted to get our orders out of the way and get down to

business. The second we were handed menus I asked the waiter what he recommended.

"Prawn casserole as a starter, followed by… "

Gönül interrupted.

"I don't eat prawns."

"What's today's special?" I asked.

"Filet mignon with mushrooms; or schnitzel."

"Which would you like?" I asked Gönül.

"Why don't we order both and share," she suggested. "That way we won't be eyeing each other's plates."

It wasn't a bad idea. We ordered. Once the waiter left, Gönül began to talk.

"As you may know, I sometimes go out on tour."

I didn't know. But it didn't seem important, so I didn't react. Still, she was determined to explain everything in detail.

"Sweetie, a real merchant knows when and where to make money. You've got to wait till the hazelnuts or cotton has been harvested. Then you call in your debts. You've got to know when they come to pick cotton in Ceyhan. That's the time to offer your services. Once the work's done, when men have empty hands and full pockets, what's on their minds? Us! So you see, I work systematically."

I had to hand it to her. I couldn't believe no one else had thought of it. If one gets past her affected lisp, her sense of technique is certainly praiseworthy.

"That's clever, all right," I complimented her.

"Of course. I know what I'm doing. The others think I'm some kind of hick, but I know every trick in the book. I won't tell you any more, though. That just won't do."

I read somewhere that people can influence the intelligence

of others nearby. Gönül is definitely one of those. Sitting across
from her, I felt my ability to think dwindle away, my IQ retreat
into double digits.

"Anyway. I headed for Rize last year just after the tea
harvest. You can't imagine how hard it is to keep track of those
things. I hear the harvest dates on TV and off I go."

The assistant waiter brings us our drinks. Gönül is quiet
until he leaves.

"So I went to Rize, wondering what my share of the tea
harvest would be. There are special coffee houses where the tea
merchants and workers hang out. I had a seat at one of them.
The air simply heaved with kismet. One day a young man
arrived. He was a handsome, well-built guy. We reached an
agreement. Off we went to his house. There were six or seven
of them, all brothers. And Yusuf was the baby of the family. I
sized him up at a glance. He was just like a girl. So beautiful.
Those eyes. Those lips. That pink complexion. As though he
was born with a powdered nose. Once his brothers were done
with me, and I was on my way, he followed me all along the
road, pestering me with questions about Istanbul, what kind of
work he could find if he came. What he was getting at was just
so obvious."

Our food arrived.

"Which one do you want to start with?" she asked.

I let her choose.

"I'll start with the wet one. Then move on to the dry one."

I carefully divided the schnitzel into two equal portions,
pushing hers to one side of my plate.

"In short, the dear boy followed me around for two days.
And I brought him to Istanbul with me."

"But he wasn't even of age. He was still a child."

"I know," she admitted. "But if I hadn't taken him with me someone else would have. He'd made up his mind. He was determined to come to Istanbul."

Her lisp had become still more exaggerated, with thin 'e's replacing most 'a's. I was concentrating so hard on her liberties with the Turkish language that I missed most of what she was saying. I mean, I was having trouble following what she was saying, even though we both speak the same language. Or at least versions of it.

"Weren't you frightened? That's like kidnapping a child."

"*Aman*, what's there to be afraid of? They marry off boys and girls that age."

"What about his older brothers? What did they do?"

"I've got no idea. We didn't call and ask."

She was totally engrossed in her meal, and speaking much more slowly as a result. First, she cut her meat into tiny pieces, then transferred her fork to her right hand. Each morsel was then conveyed to her mouth, one by one.

"He was going to be my companion. He'd go off to work with me, learn all the ropes. He'd be like a daughter. I even christened him Gül after his face, which was like a rose. The name stuck."

"He'd also make you a lot of money..."

"Naturally. In any case, he was all set to get into the business. Why shouldn't it benefit me instead of others? Don't you agree? And when he grew up he'd look after me. We'd work together, eat together. I have no intention of working the road for the rest of my life."

"Then what happened?"

"What do you think? He met that whore Ceren. My little lamb didn't have a mean bone in his body. He adored everything he saw, and wanted it. You know me. I'm careful with my money. I don't spend like crazy. The more Gül saw, the more he wanted; nothing was enough. Then Ceren got on his tail."

Her face suddenly grew bitter, lower lip twisted and distended, like Mürevvet Sim. Her eyes rolled sideways, disapprovingly.

"Ceren peddled him right and left. He was just rolling in it. A hairless boy, like a peanut. And he knew what he was doing. Who knows how many tricks a night he turned; you can imagine."

There was an unmistakable trace of envy in Gönül's voice. And she did have a point after all, she'd found the beautiful boy, brought him to the city, and then seen the cream of her efforts skimmed off by Ceren.

"Do you have any idea how he died?"

"He drowned. In a well. You know the proverb about the earthenware water jug being broken on the way to the well. Well, in this case it's true. He died as he lived."

"And Ceren died just a day earlier in a fire."

"May Allah damn her to hell! May she burn in hell! The whore got what she deserved. That disgusting bitch! What else can I say?"

"Well, she is dead," I noted.

We exchanged plates. I started on the filet mignon.

"I'm so upset about Gül," Gönül continued, mouth full. "He was just so pretty. Like his name. A beautiful face like the Prophet Joseph."

That's it! The uncanny coincidence, half registered and half hidden somewhere in the shadows of my mind, was lit up as though by a flashbulb: the similarity between what happened to Gül-Yusuf and the story of the Prophet Yusuf! Both were renowned for their beauty. Both were the youngest of a large family. With his perfect temperament and beauty, the Prophet Yusuf was the most beloved of his father's children. The Prophet Yusuf also had elder brothers. According to the Holy Book, the brothers were so jealous of their father's favouritism they cast poor Yusuf into a well. Gül also had brothers. And Gül died in a well.

The newly arrived cup of strong, black coffee brings me back to my senses. Her brothers must have found and punished her. That sort of traditional justice is still common in some parts. Families gather to pass judgement on members who have gone astray. A verdict of execution is often reached. And this particular execution is usually carried out in the most horrific way imaginable. That could be what happened to Gül, the young Yusuf. If so, it was a truly brutal act. I shuddered.

Eight

I got rid of Gönül as quickly as possible. I needed to collect my thoughts.

If Yusuf had been killed by his brothers, they could have stumbled across Ceren while tracking down Yusuf, and killed her for getting her brother mixed up in homosexuality. But Ceren died first! Well, that was possible. Perhaps they grilled her to find out where Yusuf was; they may even have tortured her to make her talk. And then they found Yusuf...

Okay so far, but even if true how could I prove it? I had nothing but a collection of hypotheses. I might be imagining the whole thing.

There was a pounding in my temples. Violence of any kind totally rattles me.

The lady doctor at the coroner's office could be of help, but that was conditional on one thing: letting her play with my arse. I could clench my jaw and let her. The worst possible scenario was failing to get any information. I'd end up with a sore bum for nothing.

If I only knew exactly what I was looking for. But I didn't.

Perhaps commissioner Selçuk Tanyer, whom I hadn't seen in ages, could be of some help. I went home and looked him up in my rolodex. He was listed on the last page under the title "police chief". Right at my fingertips.

It took some effort to reach him, but I finally did.

"Hey!" he exclaimed. "Long time no see. You only call when you need something."

There's nothing more irritating then beginning a conversation with a reproach. He acted as though my answering machine was full of messages from him. As though he'd been trying to reach me but I only thought of him when it was useful.

"I didn't wish to disturb you," I said. "I know how devoted you are to your work."

"I've always got time for you," he said.

He meant it. We were childhood friends, grew up in the same neighbourhood. He'd protect me when we played out in the street. Later, we'd suck each other's lips until they were swollen.

"How can I help you," he asked.

I summed things up for him. I knew his department had nothing to do with the case, but I hoped he'd find a way to get access to the coroner's report.

"You've got some interesting ideas," he said. "You might be right on the trail. Our fellows thought of the same thing. They may even be investigating the brothers. Give me a second and I'll find out."

"What about the coroner's report?" I asked.

"It's finished," he said. "I'll send it to you."

I'd have preferred him to suggest a policeman escort me to the forensic science building. I'd have liked to see the expression on the bottom molester's face when I arrived with an official escort.

I told him what was on my mind.

"Don't exaggerate, dear," he said. "There's no need to turn this into high drama."

I gave him my number, and we agreed to meet as soon as possible. I hate waiting. It makes me tense. I don't know what to do with myself. I feel like anything I start will end up half-done. Sitting and waiting only makes time pass even more slowly. Waiting is torture.

I decided to kill time on the computer. There are always files that need sorting, programs to be deleted. Or I could surf the net, chat, play cards at one of the game sites.

I'm a whiz at the PC. My computer is just right for me. The updates I'd added gave it an incredible performance.

I began with mindless scanning and compression tasks, first sorting through old dossiers. I found records dating back to the launch of our chat room. As I was about to delete them, I noticed the nick Jihad2000. He always ended with the formula *bismillahirrahmanirrahim*.

I got online and entered our "manly-girls" chat room. There was no sight of Jihad2000. He could be in other chat rooms. I found him by using a powerful search engine. In alphabetical order, he was in the following rooms: "Islam", "Istanbul", "Sex", "Sweethearts" and "*Zurna*". He is fast, and able to keep up with them all at once.

I asked for a private chat. He responded to my DCC request with the usual prayer formula. I asked for his help. That's how we started. I also allowed him to float prayers and the slogans he had prepared earlier. When I told him another one of us had died, he flew into a rage.

>you're all infidels! death is your salvation
heretics!
infidels who alter Allah's work

you were born men, you live as women
death is your salvation
you too are an infidel
you too will die>

I didn't understand. He was implying that some of us are immortal. I wrote:

<We'll all die one day.
Don't you agree?>

He hadn't yet begun writing in capital letters. Once his temperature had fallen, he asked what kind of help I wanted. I asked if he knew anything about the death of Yusuf-Gül.

<the prophets are unsullied
Their names are sacred
They can't be defiled
Those who do shall be punished>

I thought I caught his drift.

<don't you see?
Salih died in an earthquake
Abraham was tested in a fire
Joseph was cast into a well
The prophets' names are sacred
Those who use their names
Must be worthy
The Koran lists 25 prophets

And so much else
Each people were sent a prophet
Adam, Noah, David, Moses, Jesus, Mohammed!

And then came the trademark big, angry letters:

<THOSE WHO DEFILE THE NAMES OF PROPHETS ARE
INFIDELS THE END OF THE INFIDELS IS NIGH>

He was no longer responding to me. He was off on a bender. He'd connected to the "manly-girls" room and was floating the same messages there.

I calculated that if I was quick I would be able to find his server information, or at least where he was connected. Just as I opened the appropriate monitor program the phone rang.

It was Selçuk. He would have the coroner's report sent over the following morning. The Seçkin brothers had never come to Istanbul from their home in Rize. There was no reason to suspect them. They hadn't even attended the funeral and had told a reporter that they didn't have "a little brother like that".

"Come to dinner one evening. You'll have a chance to see Ayla."

Ayla was his wife. She was also from the neighbourhood. Selçuk had sucked her lips as well as mine. He'd preferred hers. They began going out when they were in middle school. In short, they'd been happily married for as long as I could remember.

"Allah willing," I said.

Chatting with Jihad2000 had affected my choice of words. The monitoring program had done its job. Jihad2000 had cut off his private connection to me, but it didn't matter. I'd found out where he was connected. It was just the information I needed.

I remembered a fair amount about the history of the prophets. Years ago I'd read all the holy books out of curiosity. What's more, my interest in costume films and devotion to Ava Gardner had led to my watching John Huston's "The Bible" on DVD. Adam and Eve, Cain and Abel, Nimrod, Noah's flood, Abraham, Lot, and Sodom and Gomorra stayed in my mind from the film. The most handsome man of the time, Peter O'Toole, had played the three angels that visit Lot in the sinful cities of Sodom and Gomorra.

In the film, coloured by the conservatism and censorship of the 1960s, Sodom and Gomorra was an ill-defined gloomy place. I couldn't help imagining how an imaginative director of our own times could enliven it with some well-shot porn scenes.

I had fuzzy images of the tale of the Prophet Joseph from my childhood, and remembered a film starring Yusuf Sezgin. The similarity between the names Yusuf Sezgin and Yusuf Seçkin was truly unnerving.

As far as I remembered, the Prophet Abraham was cast into a furnace by the unbelieving King Nimrod, but the flames were transformed into birds. Prophet Abraham escaped unscathed, and his followers increased. Our Abraham-Ceren had simply burned to a crisp. The flames hadn't become birds.

Jihad2000 had mentioned Salih, who was caught in a great earthquake. Who was Salih? What earthquake was it?

I began researching, and came across Prophet Salih's name. He is mentioned as one of the prophets in the Koran. He was sent to the idolatrous Arab tribe known as the Semud. He called on them to follow the one, true God. They didn't believe him, and maimed and killed a female camel sent by God. If there really was a God, they wanted to know how he would punish them. Salih told them to hide themselves in caves carved into a cliff-face. Then came a powerful storm and earthquake. The unbelievers perished in their homes.

So the Prophet Salih really did have some connection to earthquakes and storms.

But why had Jihad2000 made a sudden reference to Salih? When had a girl of ours named Salih died? I racked my brain, but came up with nothing.

I called Hasan, our all-knowing *muhtar*. He was busy, and kept it short. At first he hesitated when he heard the name, then he remembered who Salih was.

"Ah, that's right. You know her as Deniz. It happened a few months back. She fell into the elevator shaft and died."

I remembered. It hadn't been considered a suspicious death. She had indeed fallen into an elevator shaft in a district of high rises in Atakoy. I recalled it clearly. It had nothing to do with an earthquake. There had been no connection between a tremor and Deniz's death. We grieved, but quickly moved on.

"Have there been any dead girls with the real names Isa, Musa, Nuh and such?" I asked.

"What's this all about? Some kind of history of the prophets?" he asked.

Actually, that was about right. What we had here was a series of deaths that all closely followed the history of the prophets. Girls with names the same as prophets were dropping dead. What's more, there was an uncanny similarity between the way they died and the prophet after whom they were named.

I needed to wait for the reports sent by Selçuk in order to get more detailed information about Gül and Ceren, otherwise known as Yusuf and İbrahim, but that didn't stop me from investigating the death of Deniz, or Salih. I could begin looking into it, but it had been at least a few months, and the trail was certainly cold. What could I expect to find? The answer was nothing, or next to nothing.

I didn't really know Deniz. But she was a close friend of Cise, a club regular. They even lived together for a while. Then, furious at having her clothes peed on, Cise flung Deniz's poodle at the wall, and the relationship ended. Perhaps a brief chat with Cise when I went to the club this evening would result in some information.

I cleared my thoughts and went through a list of alternatives: A) I was paranoid, B) Jihad2000's ridiculous ramblings were provoking me, C) A maniacal serial killer was on the loose, D) Everything could be put down to coincidence.

Paranoia can be most beneficial: it encourages a cautious approach to life. I have yet to suffer any consequences for being paranoid. In fact, I loathe people without a dose of paranoia. How can people be so smug, so complacent? I think it's just plain silly. There is nothing healthier than a suspicious approach to at least some aspects of life. And who can deny that once you get going there's more than enough to worry about.

I automatically eliminated the alternative D. Even if it was all a coincidence, I had become involved. Even if events could be put down to a series of twists of fate, that too would have to be proven.

As far as Jihad2000, he may have been spouting nonsense. I still couldn't overlook the fact that he knew so much, and that it went so well with his master plan of damnation. It wouldn't be impossible to track him down and monitor his every move. It would be well worth it. If nothing else, I could tug his ear, frighten him, keep him from letting loose on our chat room.

The possibility that we faced a crazed serial killer was certainly an intriguing thought. And as frightening as it was intriguing. There were any number of question marks, starting with who the killer was and what motivated him or her. If he was out there, he had to be stopped dead in his tracks.

And then there was the possibility that Jihad2000 himself was the serial killer.

I examined the address he had connected from. Unsurprisingly, it was a fictitious one. It wasn't difficult for me to find his user name from his server. He had connected using the not very widespread server doruk.net, and his user name was recorded as <u>kbarutcu@doruk.net.tr.</u>

Doruk mostly targeted the corporate internet services segment. For that reason, their security systems were highly developed. That didn't mean I couldn't penetrate them, however.

I prepared myself a cup of fennel tea before getting to work. After a few sips, I decided the order in which I would tackle the tasks that lay before me. It proved much more challenging than I had expected. There were a number of needless security measures. But once I had cracked the username code the rest unravelled like a well-worn stocking.

"kbarutcu" was none other than Kemal Barutçu. He lived in Beşiktaş. I recorded his address and two registered phone numbers.

There were no details on whether it was a home address or a business address. Each would present a host of different problems. The last thing I needed was a bunch of family members or colleagues flocking around me if he wasn't alone.

A visit wouldn't necessarily be a problem, but I had to determine if I was going to a private home or a business address. I decided to call first, since it was unclear what I would face. I didn't want to call from my home phone, which would enable him to record my number. I ran my telephone decoder programme, and a number in Jersey was chosen at random. My number would appear to be this number. And the call would be recorded on the telephone bill of whoever this person in Jersey was.

The phone didn't ring for long. "*Efendim*?" answered a nasal voice on the other end. The voice was insecure, young and clearly male. I was pleased to have been right about his age.

"Kemal *Bey*, please," I said.

"Speaking. How can I help you?"

He sounded educated, but mumbled.

"Excuse me, could you tell me if I have reached a private home or a business?"

"Where are you calling from?"

The voice instantly became peevish.

"We are conducting a survey on internet services," I informed him.

"Yes?"

"Home or business?" I repeated.

"Home," he replied.

I'd obtained the information I was after. There was no need to drag it out. I thanked him and hung up.

It was time to pay a call on Kemal Barutçu, he of the peevish voice and alias Jihad2000. If nothing else, I intended to give him a fright over his behaviour in the chat room. It would be just as well if I took the opportunity to inform him personally that using a nickname did not prevent me from learning his real identity and that he would be in big trouble if he persisted in annoying me.

Ten

I put on my most masculine outfit, and, quite the trendy young man, off I went to Akdoğan Sokak, a street parallel to Barbaros Bulvarı in Beşiktas. To one side was a row of nondescript buildings on "The Street of the Beloved". I didn't think much of the name.

The apartment building was grey, worn, and squeezed into the row. The street door was locked, and there was no front door bell or doorman. I pressed the bell for apartment #2. When nothing happened, I pressed it again. It opened.

The hallway was dim and smelled of mildew. Apartment #2 was on the first floor. From within, echoed a woman's voice.

"Who is it?"

The classic response "me" usually works well enough. I decided against it, not wanting to panic the woman inside. I wondered what to say. Somehow I had always imagined Kemal himself opening the door.

As I sprinted up the stairs I shouted out, "I'm looking for Kemal Barutçu."

Before I'd even finished, I was in front of the door.

A short woman wearing a headscarf stood in the doorway. It was probably his mother. Her dark blue eyes looked at me inquisitively, but without suspicion.

"Who are you?" she asked.

"I'm looking for Kemal Barutçu," I repeated. "Is he at home?"

"Yes," she said. "I mean, where else could he be?"

"I'm a friend from the internet," I added. It was a white lie, at worst.

She opened the door wider to let me in.

"Come in, my son," she said. "Kemal is inside, in his room."

I hesitated over whether or not to remove my shoes. If I needed to flee for any reason it would be best to keep them on my feet. I wiped them thoroughly on the doormat.

"Come in, come in," she said.

It was a comfortable flat. The furniture had clearly been purchased on an instalment plan from the local shop. There were no details of any note. Actually, there was: the relative lack of furniture. These sorts of homes are usually jam-packed with furnishings; this one was half-empty. What's more, there weren't any carpets or *kilims* covering the floor, which was linoleum with a parquet design.

It looked nothing like the home of a religious fanatic. The walls weren't covered with calligraphic sermons; the corners weren't full of open Arabic books on lecterns and prayer rugs.

The door we knocked on opened into a room overlooking the park. It was brightly lit. Kemal Barutçu sat at his computer, his back to us. In a wheelchair!

When his mother touched his shoulder, he turned. Looking me straight in the eye was Stephen Hawking's Istanbul version. He smiled, revealing pink gums.

"*Merhaba*," he greeted me.

His arms looked healthy. He extended one for a handshake.

"I was expecting you," he said. "But you're a bit late..."

It was now my turn to look puzzled.

"Mother, go make us some tea," he asked. "With some cookies, if there are any."

His mother left without a word.

"Close the door," he said. "My mother eavesdrops."

I obeyed.

I looked for a place to sit. Other than the wheelchair, the only place was the bed. He gestured for me to sit down on it. He turned his wheelchair so he was facing me. I saw intelligence in his alert expression.

"You're late in finding me," he began. "You almost disappointed me. I knew you were monitoring me. That's how I knew you'd come."

"I don't understand," I said.

"I've been monitoring you, too," he said. He tried, and failed, to wink at me from behind his thick glasses. "I'm a real fan. You know what I mean."

So, he'd been tracking me, and I hadn't even realised. As I always say, no matter what security precautions you take, anyone determined to trace you over the internet can. The living proof of this sat across from me.

"I had no idea," I admitted.

"Of course not," he said. "I'm amazed by your computer skills. I've been following you. You've developed your own signature. Allah permitting, I will too one day."

Out of the corner of my eye, I glanced at the equipment spread over his desk. It was extensive. He had the infrastructure to do just about anything he wished.

"You know what," he smiled. "You're nothing like what I imagined."

I hadn't exactly expected someone stuck in a wheelchair, either. Considering what he'd written, the force with which he'd condemned us all, it hadn't even seemed a remote possibility.

He cackled, which made him sound like a child.

"So you found me!" he cried.

Pitying him, I almost forgot my anger. On the other hand, the fact that he was a cripple didn't necessarily make him an angel, nor did it prevent him from causing trouble. Our tea and apple cookies dusted with powdered sugar arrived.

He had an unusual mind. He knew all about most of the work I'd done. While he admired my skills, even looking up to me as some kind of role model, he also considered me to be a rival. I worked mainly for international corporations, but he had chosen as his employers companies with a radical Islamist bent. He had enjoyed some success preparing security systems and web designs for them. That said, he hadn't yet made a name for himself on the market, and consequently charges less than me.

As a result of this combination of envy and admiration, he had researched me at length. While I have nothing much too hide, it still didn't seem quite right for a housebound person in a wheelchair to have learned so much about me.

He had been crippled from birth, the result of a marriage between relatives. His parents, criticised for what they'd done, had no more children. He had been so badly teased that despite winning a place he didn't go to university. Computer work was ideal; he didn't even have to get up.

He wasn't a graduate of a religious school, as I'd assumed. But his faith in Islam was unwavering. While he didn't meet all the obligations of his beliefs, he observed as many as possible.

He believed he had been born as divine punishment for his parents. We are all on this earth to be tested. He was his parent's test. With Kemal's birth they had closed themselves off, cutting nearly all social ties, but had succeeded admirably in raising him. While they weren't as devout as their son, their relative lack of piety had done nothing to dampen his. They were determined to raise their one and only child as a true believer in Islam, and did all in their power to do so. First, they hired an elderly woman who had visited Mecca, then a *hoca* was employed to give him religious lessons. After a certain age, he was able to educate himself.

His father was a bank inspector, and often out of town on business. When he was home, he was usually too tired to take much of an interest in his son.

The cookies were delicious, filled with fruit. I would be in real trouble if I kept gobbling them down. In any case, I was binging these days. I gain weight every autumn. It's my body's way, every year, of preparing me for winter.

From what Kemal told me, he didn't reserve a particular enmity for transvestites. They were on a par with the other sinners and unbelievers: gays, lesbians, Jews, socialists, the immodestly dressed, drinkers of alcohol, and those who fail to teach their children to fast and pray. There were so many who failed the test, who strayed from the path of righteousness and were infidels. I belonged to a minor sub-category.

The messages he sent on the internet had no particular relevance. He wrote the same things, no matter what chat room he was in. No one could stop him. It wasn't their place to do so. He was simply inviting everyone to the path of righteousness. It was up to his readers to obey, or not.

He was a total homosexual. While he didn't confess as much, that was my objective evaluation. His general lack of confidence, coupled with occasional bursts of overconfidence, the mimics and gestures he used when explaining something, the sideways glance as he said it was "not their place" to stop him. Considering his condition, it was highly unlikely he had ever done anything, nor likely that he ever would. He chatted on quite merrily about sinners, infidels and whatnot, but when condemning homosexuality a certain gleam in his eye gave him away.

Up to a point, his hostility was perfectly reasonable. I understood. While everyone else was living it up, he couldn't do a thing. He never had and he would never be able to. I'm sure he had practically memorised all the internet porn sites. Seeing as he was online all day, he had certainly visited them. It was easy to imagine the sighs as he stared at his monitor, the loathing and rebellion when he then looked at himself in the mirror.

"You're a real beauty like these two," he complimented me. "I was able to intercept two photos you sent to a friend over the net. You were wearing a leather mini-skirt."

That's right. I had those taken at Ipek's birthday party. Then I e-mailed them to my friends. So he'd even got his hands on them. I didn't think much of myself in those snapshots. I looked like Vampirella, a heroine of my childhood comic books, or maybe a sexier version of Angelica Huston in *The Addams Family*.

"You had long hair," he said.

"It was a wig."

"You were wearing high-heel boots," he continued.

"I don't really go out like that," I told him. "Just at night."

"That's all right," he said. "You're beautiful like this too."

I had arrived in my most convincing "young man about town" costume, but there was no dampening his enthusiasm. Kemal was ready to be seduced. Just one experience could change his life, his outlook, everything. Now, I wasn't about to make such a sacrifice for nothing. The last thing I needed was to do something that would later haunt my dreams.

I told him what I was after. Unlike during chat, all traces of impulsive behaviour had evaporated. He simply listened, making tiny cries of protest. As I spoke, he stared at my mouth. I didn't appreciate it, as I prefer eye contact, so long as it is not exaggerated.

He suddenly snarled at me.

"I don't know anything. But good on whoever was responsible! They deserved it!"

Now, that sort of talk really pisses me off. I lose my temper. Without meaning to, I struck him full across the face. It was reflexive. I was ashamed of myself.

But then I noticed a spark of desire in his eyes. I changed my mind. I had a complete masochist on my hands. He continued raining insults, not raising his voice, so his mother wouldn't hear.

"I'm glad it happened. Faggots! Infidels!" he hissed.

I was undecided on whether or not to slap him again. I waited. He looked at me hungrily.

I've encountered masochists before, but none of them were cripples. Sadomasochists are a widespread subset of the gay community. What they practise is known simply as S&M, which also stands for slave-master. S&M was not one of my interests. I did have some knowledge of it though, from films and websites.

I grabbed a fistful of thick, wavy hair and jerked his head back. He held his breath. I spit in his face.

"You piece of shit!" I too had taken to hissing. He looked at me with wide, astonished eyes. His tongue crept out and onto his lips, licking off my saliva. His eyes pleaded for me. His lower lip drooped and his mouth hung half open.

I leaned over, my face inches from his, and stared him directly in the eye.

"You," I said, "are a complete maniac!"

"I am!" he agreed.

His voice trembled with excitement. Without hesitation I once more spit in his face. This time, it landed on his quivering lips.

His hand had strayed to his crotch. He seemed to be in a state of stunned disbelief, acting only on his animal instincts.

I reached out, grabbed his hand and raised it.

"There'll be none of that!" I commanded. The master lurking within me had come to life. I caught him sneaking his other hand towards his crotch. Invalids often have strong arms, but he was no match for me.

"Again . . . Please . . . " he begged.

I dropped his arm and slapped him again, so hard saliva sprayed from his lips. The hand returned. He was about to come. I had no idea how to help him climax.

I squeezed his nipples. It wasn't easy to find them through his thick sweatshirt. In fact, I wasn't sure I was even pinching my intended target. But he pushed his chest out.

His eyelids fluttered wildly. As a final act of assistance, I smacked him once more. And, he came.

His sweatpants were stained. He looked at me with a stunned expression.

Men with problems tend to regret everything once they've climaxed. They run home to repent alone. Others are filled with hatred, and take it out on their partners. They are the ones I truly fear. There's nothing they won't do to suppress their sense of shame and guilt. Some will kill.

I didn't know what to expect from Kemal. I read regret in his eyes. But also detected relaxation and pleasure.

"You were good," he said.

So he enjoyed it. And he didn't seem at all ashamed.

"We have sinned," he said.

"So you realise it's a sin," I teased.

"We're all sinners," he replied. "What's the point of being on this earth if we are incapable of sin?"

I couldn't believe my ears. What was this transformation?

He begged me to visit him again. He told me that we could arrange for his mother to be out, that we would be all alone and able to get undressed next time. For a moment, I thought I'd feel sick. But I didn't.

I made him promise not to cause any more problems in our chat room. I threatened him, warning him that if he did, his address and everything we did today would soon be posted on the internet. He got the message. I had nothing to hide. He did.

I ordered him to do some research into the girls' deaths, and to let me know if he came up with anything. Then, and only then, would I consider a second visit.

Finally, I told him that I would pass along any computer work that wasn't worth my while. We agreed on that as well.

He wanted to kiss me goodbye. Now that I knew what turned him on, I denied him the pleasure. I even considered a parting slap. In the end, I pressed a knee into his chest and grabbed his chin. I jerked it upwards. He held his breath.

I glared into his eyes. He waited expectantly. For what, even I didn't know.

I released his chin roughly. His head bobbed sideways.

"Please come again," he called after me. "If you don't, I've got plans of my own."

Eleven

There's no question that wheelchair-bound Kemal has exotic tastes, and suffers from a guilt complex. He is also hostile and blindly devoted to his religion. But he is no killer.

Dusk had fallen as I left Kemal's house. It was turning into a long and eventful day. When I arrived home, my answering machine was full of messages.

The first one was from Ayla, who had called just to hear my voice. She said she hoped to see me soon, and hung up. As always, ever since our childhood, I detected a hint of aggression in her voice. It was ridiculous of her to feel jealous after so many years. What was there to resent, anyway? Selçuk had chosen her over me, and they were married. What else did she want?

Next came a call from Hasan. He sounded agitated, told me he had a bombshell to drop and asked me to call right back.

Then came Ponpon in a panic. She said Hasan had called her, adding that she couldn't believe what I was getting mixed up in. The message made no sense.

Of all the girls, Ponpon is the one I like best. She's cultured and funny. For as long as I can remember she has been doing drag shows at major hotels. She also keeps busy with private performances. Birthday parties, special celebrations and even circumcision ceremonies.

"What can I do?" she says. "If they want to circumcise their sons, and then, once they've become men, have them spend the night with me, just what am I supposed to do? I thank my fellow citizens."

I wasn't used to hearing panic in her voice, since she's a cheerful and sometimes even slightly callous sort.

Ali seems to pride himself on calling me every time I prepare to leave the house. This was no exception. He wanted to discuss a proposal he'd received from a German company, Frechen Gmbh, and told me to call him back no matter what the hour. His tone made it clear that there were loads of money to be made. Ali is the sort of man who suddenly speaks with a whole new sense of confidence when money will soon be entering his pocket.

In short, all the callers but Ayla expected me to phone them back.

I gave Ponpon top billing.

"Where on earth were you, *ayol*!" she began.

"What's going on?"

"What do you think, sweetie? That Hasan of yours has my head spinning. I'm virtually unhinged as it is, so you can imagine what it's done to me."

"What is it?"

"There's some sort of pervert, or a whole gang of them. Something dangerous. Our girls are getting killed. You've uncovered them. But you don't know who they are."

Hasan had let his imagination run away with him once again. What he said might turn out to be true, but I hadn't yet put the pieces together quite that way. I wondered if he'd found out anything new, remembering his claim to have some news of a "bombshell".

"I'm not sure of anything yet," I said. "Nothing's that certain. I've just got a lot of suspicions."

"That's not what Hasan said!"

"I haven't talked to him yet. He may have found out something else. Believe me when I say I don't know any more. Anyway, why are you in such a panic?"

"My name is Zekeriya!"

"So?"

"What do you mean 'so'? Zekeriya is the name of a prophet. If what Hasan says is true, and there's some maniac serial killer who's chasing after people named after prophets, I'm next in line."

I'd known Ponpon for years, but only as Ponpon. I'd even forgotten that she must have had a real name.

"Sweetie, I'm absolutely terrified! That Hasan of yours has scared me to death. I can't possibly go to the hotel alone. I've got to find someone to go with me. Anyway, that's not my main problem. There's no way I'm staying home on my own!"

"Don't exaggerate, Ponpon," I reassured her.

"I'm not exaggerating, *ayol*. I'm not some sheep to be led to the slaughter. You've got to understand. I'm terrified. I wouldn't be caught dead on my own at a time like this!"

"All right, come stay with me if you want."

"I'll be right over. I'll go to the hotel, finish work and then head straight for your place. I'm totally frazzled. I can't even sit down."

"Fine," I said. "You're welcome to come. I'm here at home."

When she hung up I called Hasan. His line was busy, as usual. It was to be expected. How else could he spread so many rumours in such a short time to so many people? The salary I pay him can't possibly cover his phone bill. He must rake in the tips.

I decided to try Ali later. He was sure to keep me on the phone for ages, and I had no intention of talking endlessly about work. About a German company no less.

I loathe German porn. It's the epitome of bad taste; the most repulsive sex imaginable – crooked, straight, wet and dry. It seems calculated to put people off sex for good. There's never a single beautiful woman, handsome man or presentable boy in German films. Not to mention that the soles of the feet of the performers are inevitably filthy. It's just disgusting.

I tried Hasan again. The line was still busy.

The doorbell rang. It was Ponpon, who lives two streets up the hill. She must have jumped into her car the second she hung up. She carried an enormous wardrobe bag full of clothes on hangers.

"*Ayol*, give me a hand," she demanded. "I've got two more."

She seemed to be moving in with me for good. The bags she'd referred to were enormous suitcases. She couldn't have packed them in such a short time. Clearly, she'd arranged everything before calling me, including getting her things ready.

She was wearing stage makeup. On her head was a knotted old stocking, in preparation for a wig. Naturally, during her performances, she went through several changes of costume and wigs, and the stocking was one of the tricks of the trade.

She settled into my guest room. I watched.

"What's with the staring?" she asked. "Is something wrong with my makeup?"

"No," I replied. "I was just watching you. I was lost in thought."

Not content with my answer, she raced to the full-length mirror, and examined herself under the spotlight. She caressed

and rearranged her entire body. Then posed. She raised, then
lowered, an eyebrow. She sucked in the hollows of her cheeks.
In short, she did all any self-respecting girl would do under the
circumstances. Still, she wasn't convinced.

"You don't think it's a bit much."

She pointed to her eye-shadow. As far as I'm concerned, she
applies too much makeup, but that's her style. Considering she
would be up on stage, it was really quite moderate.

"Not at all," I said. "It's just fine."

"All right then. I've really got to go. I've got some business
on the side to take care of first."

"Fine," I said.

"Where should I go when I'm finished tonight? Home or the
club?"

"Wherever you like," I told her. "Here are the spare keys. I'll
be at the club."

"Well aren't we feeling all carefree and light-hearted, *ayol*!"

She blew me two kisses and sped off with mincing little steps.

I called Hasan again. This time I got through.

"Where have you been," he began. "I've got the most
amazing news!"

"I've been at home. But your number's always busy."

"I've got the most incredible news!"

"So you say. Go on then," I said.

"I'm terrified you won't believe me."

"Hasan, stop dragging it out. Everyone believes you.
Ponpon's in a total panic. She's moved in with me."

"Of course. She should be," he said. "After all, she's named
Zekeriya. What a funny name! I didn't think there were any
more of those around. Seems I was wrong. And of all the

people to be named Zekeriya!"

"Hasan, I'm telling you for the last time. Get to the point."

"Listen," he said. "Your theory seems to be right on the mark. Something's happening to the girls named after prophets. There were three more of them recently. Their names are Musa, Yunus and – hold on to your wig – Muhammet!"

"Muhammet?"

"Yes, from Iran."

"Why didn't we hear anything about it?" I asked.

"There's no way we'd have heard about it? It happened so far away. Muhammet was working in Van, one of those transvestites who fled Iran and found refuge in Turkey. They say they were victims of the regime. But they're real popular over in East Turkey. Guess what happened."

"I'll never guess. Just tell me."

"It's no fun telling you anything," he complained.

"Fun? We're talking about a murdered Iranian girl here."

"You're right. I guess I got carried away."

Hasan was out of line, but he came to his senses. Or at least dispensed with the giddy, self-important airs.

"Anyway," he continued. "She disappeared a while ago. Her friends – it seems she wasn't alone – reported her missing to the police. Then they found her body in a cave up in the mountains. Some shepherds found it. It was unrecognisable. They said it had probably been eaten by wild animals, wolves and jackals and the like. The police didn't bother to investigate. The thing is: what was she doing up in the mountains? From what they say, she was a delicate slip of a thing. So what was she doing in some mountain cave?

That knocked the wind out of me. I don't just get upset by

news like this. I feel like my insides are being torn out.

"Are you there?"

"Yes," I said. "Sorry. I guess I lost it."

"If you'd prefer I'll tell you the rest at the club."

"You'd better give me a quick rundown now," I said. You can leave the details for later."

"All right," he said. "Musa was from Antalya. Born and bred. He hadn't even bothered to change his name. And there's another incredible detail: he stuttered!"

I remembered that the Prophet Musa had some kind of speech defect, and that his brother Harun acted as his spokesman.

"This really is too much," I exclaimed.

"It's not over! I think she was the first to die. It's been a year or so."

"So how did Musa die?" I asked.

She was found dead on a winter day in an abandoned mountain cabin. They never determined the cause," he replied.

"And you mentioned Yunus..."

"That's right, I was about to forget her," he said. "She was working the motorway out on TEM, but went missing at the beginning of summer. She was known as Funda."

"Was her body found in the sea? The Prophet Yunus was swallowed by a whale,"

"I don't know. She's still missing and there's no news."

"That's enough," I said.

"We'll talk at the club," he said. "When are you coming?"

"I won't be too late."

Were we facing a serial killer? It seemed a maniac was systematically stalking girls named after prophets.

Twelve

You could cut the air in the club with a knife. Hasan had done his bit, telling everyone he could everything he'd found out. Like all slow nights, the girls didn't have much to keep them busy. There was plenty of time for speculation. Hasan had panicked everyone at the club, relating every gruesome detail for those he'd been unable to reach on the phone.

Osman contributed to the general tension by playing edgy music. The same minimal melody blared out over and over. It was enough to make anyone jumpy, even if they weren't already suffering a case of the jitters.

The lights were turned up higher than usual. The usual pleasant murkiness was gone, replaced by a disturbingly naked luminosity.

Şükrü mournfully tended bar. He perched on a bar stool, something I hadn't seen him do for ages. Normally, he's as alert as a flea At most, he leans on the bar. His posture spoke volumes about how low his spirits had sunk. Naturally, my Virgin Mary wasn't ready. I decided not to make an issue of it.

"Finally!" Sırma greeted me at the door. "*Abla*, we've got to talk."

I've never liked being addressed as "big sister" by those younger than me, even much younger than me. What's more,

Sırma was older. But there was enough tension already. I let it pass. It just wasn't worth pursuing.

"This sicko killer business is just the pits," said tubby Mujde. As always, she drawled out the last word in her sentence.

Hasan contributed to the general gloom by observing that "there still aren't any customers".

The girls had dispensed with their falsettos and were using their most baritone voices. The silence that had greeted my entry was replaced by a deep buzzing, as they all began talking at once.

"What is it? I demanded. "What do you want me to do?"

"I don't know," said Neslihan. "But how can we work under these conditions?"

"What's this about some pervert out on the loose?" said Elvan. "I don't believe any of it."

Elvan was a dear girl, but a bit slow. She had loudly declared that she didn't believe in AIDS, either. As though it were a question of faith. In any case, we managed to teach her, through a great deal of bossing and bullying, that she'd better protect herself.

"What about closing the club for the night and having a meeting," suggested Cise. "In any case, no one's here."

When I heard Cise's voice behind me I remembered to ask her about Deniz, who was found dead in Ataköy. But I decided that it'd be best to wait until later, seeing how wound up everyone was.

"We'll put a notice on the door," Pamir agreed.

I realised they'd been discussing everything and had decided on a plan of action long before I arrived.

There was a general air of rebellion. There was no way the

girls could work, even if they wanted to. It wasn't as though shutting up the club for one night would bankrupt us. At most, I'd just pay the boys for the night. But I was truly pissed off at Hasan. It was he who was responsible for the panic. In a sense, it was all his fault. He'd pay for it. That much was certain.

I agreed with all their suggestions. Cüneyt carefully wrote out the words "We are closed tonight and apologise for the inconvenience" on a piece of paper, and hung it up on the door. Then he added "The Management" on the bottom right hand corner.

The lights were turned up even higher. One of the girls scolded Osman, and the minimalist music was turned off. They all gathered on the dance floor, with me standing in the middle. Hasan darted to my side. He wasn't about to be left out! With me at centre stage, it was just like Hasan to try to hog some of the limelight. As the person in the eye of the storm he'd created, he began speaking first.

Every couple of sentences he was interrupted by one of the girls, with everyone else then chiming in. Each girl had some detail to add. Some knew the deceased, others knew something different about someone else. Even if they weren't directly acquainted, they'd heard things. Male names weren't really in use among us, in fact they weren't used at all except as an insult, so it took some time to connect the dots.

"Look," I said. "These names are pretty common. It could all be a coincidence."

Pamir jumped in. "You've got to be kidding! How do you explain the way they were murdered?"

"I don't know," I admitted. "I'm just trying to calm everyone down."

"We know that," said Cise. "But we've got to do something. There has to be something we can do."

Despite all the petty infighting, the girls are pretty good when it comes to a show of solidarity. Especially when it comes to a vicious customer, a conservative neighbourhood or some other outside threat. Cise is a ringleader at times like that. She's a born leader, but some of the others choose to play the helpless female.

"Cise, dear," I encouraged her. "Then let's begin with what happened to Deniz. Tell us about her."

Everyone chipped in with some scraps of information. The girls managed to fill in most details. Much of what emerged seemed highly meaningful, but so much else seemed totally random and unrelated.

We identified the first case as Musa, in Antalya. He had died about ten months earlier. The body was found in a summer house up in the mountains in early winter, at a time when everyone had migrated to their winter homes. The summer places in Antalya aren't exactly what you'd call houses. They're more like wooden shacks perched on stilts. We had no information about the cause of death. She wasn't old, but no one knew her exact age. None of the girls knew much at all about Musa. Anything they'd heard had been second-hand.

The only connection we were able to make was the name Musa and the fact that she stuttered.

Funda, whose real name was Yunus, was the next victim. Some of the girls knew her, if not well. She was beautiful, but incredibly ignorant, which meant she'd only ever been able to make a living out on the motorway. She was a loner, in every sense of the word.

The only connection seemed to be her name. What's more,

there was no proof that she was dead. She'd just disappeared. She could have moved to another city, shacked up with someone, or there were any of a number of other possibilities to explain her absence. Loneliness could even have led her to give up her transvestite lifestyle, or to commit suicide.

The only relevant bit of information was her name, Yunus. According to the Holy Book, a giant fish swallowed Yunus, but he survived in its belly for years.

It seemed impossible to establish a connection between Musa's death and the disappearance of Funda-Yunus. One was in Antalya, the other in Istanbul. The incidents were about six months apart.

Then there was Deniz, or Salih, who'd fallen into an elevator shaft in Ataköy. It'd be easy enough to find something dubious, but Deniz was known to be absent-minded, even careless. It was Jihad2000 who'd raised my suspicions. How he'd learned about it was a mystery. But, considering just how much he did know, it was hardly surprising.

She could have been pushed, or her body dumped in the shaft, but there was next to no evidence that we were dealing with a murder victim.

The name Salih didn't really come to mind when thinking of prophets. It seemed like we were forcing the connection. According to the Koran, Salih was put through the twin trials of earthquake and flood in order to test his faith. Salih and the true believers survived by taking refuge in their mountain caves, but the non-believers perished.

Deniz-Salih hadn't died at home. Her death was officially an accident. There had been no investigation into the cause of death.

From this point onwards, deaths seem to occur more frequently.

Two weeks earlier the Iranian transvestite Muhammet had disappeared in Van; her body was discovered in a cave in the mountains. The corpse had been mutilated by wild animals, and was barely recognisable. The question was: how did she die? For whatever reason, she'd been in the cave. She may have fallen asleep. She could have died of fear when wolves attacked, or they could have killed her. It's also possible that the killer murdered her first, then left her body in the cave, where it was eaten by animals. The girls were most terrified by this possibility. For that very reason, it was their favourite version.

The only thing we knew about Muhammet is that he was young, dark and applied heavy eyeliner. His name appeared to be the only bit of relevant information.

Then there was Ceren, or İbrahim, who'd burned to death in a fire, the cause of which was unknown.

And Gül, or Yusuf, who'd been found drowned in an unused well in a neighbourhood he'd never before visited.

Each of the murders could have been just an accident or due to natural causes. We had very little evidence to prove with any certainty that there was a serial killer on the loose.

Yes, there seemed to be some common themes. Their names, their youth; the fact that they were all under twenty-five years of age seemed noteworthy.

In contrast to Hasan's efforts to add fuel to the fire, to whip the girls up into a frightened frenzy, I tried my best to soothe them. I was even fairly successful at doing so.

As we sifted through the evidence, there was a pounding on the door. Cüneyt went to take a look. Ponpon had finished her performance. She was still wearing her stage costume, a totally out of fashion powder-blue evening gown. It was part of her latest act, a Muazzez Ersoy impersonation. Even the wig was the same. In other words, she was a taller, more muscular version of the lady herself.

She looked completely distraught. Although Ponpon was not a frequent visitor, all the girls at the club knew her. When they asked what was wrong, she struck her most dramatic pose.

"I'm petrified."

With a gesture that illustrated the extent of her fear, she stroked the base of her wig. Her eyes sought Hasan. When they found him, she pointed with her index finger.

"It's all because of him."

The girls laughed nervously. The fact that they were able to laugh at all showed that they were feeling better.

"Even *I* had forgotten: my real name is Zekeriya. That blabbermouth over there..."

The finger shook at Hasan.

"At first I didn't believe him when he said that girls named after prophets were being bumped off. Then, when I thought about it, I decided he may be right. I fear for my very life, of course. I'm utterly terrified."

Pamir stepped in.

"There's no reason to be scared Ponpon. The victims have all been young. I mean, clearly you're in no danger!"

This could have been interpreted as an official invitation to battle. Thank God Ponpon was able to take a joke. She laughed dryly. I know that laugh; she uses it to buy time. She'd come up with something. I've never known Ponpon not to reply in kind.

"Fine," she said. "I suppose I'm safe enough."

She moved closer to Pamir.

"But what are you going to do, Yahya *Bey*?" she asked.

I'd forgotten Pamir was named Yahya. At the mention of her male name, Pamir froze.

"What do you mean," she stammered.

"Just in case you don't remember, let me remind you. The Prophet Yahya. That is, John the Baptist. You know, the one who had his head cut off."

Ponpon made a slicing motion across her throat. As she did so, she rolled her eyes and stuck out her tongue.

Pamir was shaken enough.

"What's more, you're about the right age," added Ponpon. She then turned to the group of girls. "You do recall the story of Salome the dancer, and how she was rewarded with Yahya's head on a platter. Surely you remember?"

There was no need to make a long night even longer, to add any further to the tension. I sent everyone home. Those who wished could seek, and perhaps even find, their fortunes elsewhere tonight.

Ponpon and I went home.

Thirteen

It was well after midnight, but still far too early for me to stay at home. Ponpon, on the other hand, had given two performances, staying up on stage for an hour at each. She was tired, and for her it was late.

It was as though she was too worn out to feel afraid, and being with me had given her a sense of security and ease. She removed her makeup, singing along to the haunting Sezen Aksu song "*Yanarım*", except she'd changed the chorus to "*Yalarım*", and the words were now an explicit ode to sucking rather than a heart-rending description of deep anguish. We were both feeling a bit frazzled. I ended up laughing and singing along to this more inviting version of the dark ditty.

When Ponpon finished she announced, "Sweetie, I'm off to bed," and disappeared.

I didn't feel at all drowsy. Even if I had, there'd be no point in trying to get a good night's sleep with so many thoughts spinning through my head. I ran through my to-do list: A) Get online; B) Go investigate the housing site in Atakoy where Deniz died; C) Call Cengiz and arrange to spend the night in his arms; D) Locate Jihad2000 and find out what else he knew about the deaths.

Ponpon yelled from her bedroom:

"Turn off the lights already; how am I supposed to sleep, *ayol*!"

Instead of turning off the lights, I closed the door to the corridor. If the lights and noise were keeping Ponpon from sleeping, the problem had been neatly eliminated. I decided that going to Ataköy would be better than staying at home. If I really felt like it, I could always stop in on Cengiz on the way home.

I put on a black sweater and black spandex trousers. It seemed appropriately mysterious for such late night business. In any case, it was definitely required wearing in every film I'd ever seen. I called the taxi rank and asked for Hüseyin. I figured he may as well earn some money. He was eager to get mixed up in things like this, and I knew he'd be thrilled.

As I was tying my shoe laces, Hüseyin arrived at the door. He stood there with a bashful expression on his face, clearly hoping to be invited inside.

"*Merhaba*," he said.

"We're going to Ataköy," I informed him mischievously.

His face fell. It was a classic case of expectations being dashed by reality. I closed the door, and led the way down the staircase. I was, of course, fully aware that the spandex clung to my hips and thighs like a second skin. I permitted him to bathe me with his eyes.

"What's going on?" he wondered. "You home at this hour?"

"I've closed the club for the night," I replied.

"Are you going to go visit someone?"

His voice quavered with insecurity as he asked me this.

"No," I said. "I'll explain everything on the road."

By the time we'd made our way along the coast road to the

block of flats, I'd briefed him about Deniz's death, revealing only what he needed to know. We finally found apartment block A-18 in the middle of several high-rises in B Block. Each building was separated into Block A and Block B, with two lifts in each block. It was late, and most lights had long since been turned off; even those people still sitting up had probably nodded off by now. I reviewed my main reason for coming here in the first place: to speak to Deniz's neighbours! To extract information from the doorman...

That would be impossible. No one was around. I began examining the dozens of doorbells lining both sides of the main entrance.

"What are we looking for?" Hüseyin asked.

"I don't know."

I really didn't. Some intuition or instinct had drawn me here tonight. I didn't know what it was, or what would happen.

"You're really something!" Hüseyin exclaimed.

As I checked the doorbells to the right of the main door, he read out the names on the left hand side. It served no purpose but that of confusing me.

Most of the names seemed familiar. They were all Turkish. No surprise there. We were suddenly lit up by headlights from a car pulling into the parking lot. Looking, no doubt, like a common criminal, I turned and watched the car as it was parked. The light reminded me of being under interrogation at police headquarters. I did everything but shield my face with raised arm, guiltily turning my head to the side.

If asked who we were looking for, what would we say? If I mentioned one of the names on the doorbells, and that person turned out to be home, how would I explain? What's more, the slinky catsuit I'd selected as tonight's costume would hardly inspire a sense of trust. I had to do something. But what?

I grabbed Hüseyin, pulled him down out of the headlights, locked him in a tight embrace and began kissing him. What the boy would think, and how I would keep him in line later, were matters to be dealt with another time. There was a chance that if we seemed to be a passionately entwined couple whoever came would be too embarrassed to do anything but make a beeline straight for the door.

I kept one eye on the now darkened car, and an ear out for the sound of approaching footsteps or the clang of a closing door – my lips glued to Hüseyin's all the while. He seemed puzzled at first, but without skipping a beat he played his role to perfection. I firmly removed the hand cupping my bottom and placed it on my waist.

The car contained a couple with a baby. It took them some time to get out of their darkened vehicle. They were trying not to wake up the baby, and spoke in loud whispers. I heard every word. I may have surrendered my body, but my mind was far from the embrace of Hüseyin.

The couple entered A Block without coming anywhere near us. I immediately gave Hüseyin a shove.

"That's enough!"

"You did seem to be going all cold on me."

"I used you as camouflage," I explained.

"I thought so," he said, shaking his head.

I continued inspecting the bells. Surely my instincts had not drawn me here only to be caught by a couple with a baby or to throw myself into Hüseyin's arms. Staying where he was, Hüseyin continued reading the names aloud, but this time in a low voice. It was as entertaining as leafing through the telephone book.

"Kızılyıldız," he said. "People sure have strange names. Instead of writing it out, they've drawn a picture of a red star."

"Perhaps they're former communists," I suggested.

He continued muttering to himself as he read out the names. I went to his side to have a look. Yes, someone had sprayed a star design with red paint. It had faded.

Hüseyin seized the opportunity to seize me.

"I think someone's coming," he said.

No one was arriving or leaving. I shook him off. If he persisted, he would find himself flung head over heels into the nearby bushes. He didn't.

It suddenly hit me: Adem Yıldız, adamstar, starman, *adam, the red star! . . . Maybe we were on to something after all. My eyes shone with excitement. I felt a jolt of adrenalin. The man had seemed like a real creep. He was clearly trouble. What's more, he'd arrived at the club with Ahmet Kuyu, which spoke volumes. Ahmet Kuyu's reputation as a sadist was known to all. As Hasam suggested, the relationship between the two men could involve much more than the Yıldız brand biscuits and *börek* sponsorship of Ahmet Kuyu's new TV series. If Ahmet Kuyu was a sadist, Adem Yıldız could very well be a maniacal killer.

There was no way to know what inspired him to kill. But he was plainly a sick individual.

I sat on the stairs and collected my thoughts. Why would someone so wealthy and well-known resort to murder? If indeed he had, how could I find proof? Where was the evidence? Simply saying I was acting on a hunch just wouldn't cut it. What had I found out so far? Nothing! I had stumbled on a doorbell with a red star. It may or may not have belonged to Adem Yıldız. It was easy enough to find out. But even if it was his apartment, what would that prove?

The deaths, or murders if that's what they were, had taken place far apart. If Adem Yıldız had been anywhere near any of the crime scenes, that would go a long way towards implicating him. But it still proved nothing conclusive.

Anyway, men like him always employed others who were willing to take the rap. If things started getting sticky one of them would pop up and "confess" to all the murders.

Even if I was on the right track, I had to come up with some concrete evidence. I couldn't think of a way to implicate Adem Yıldız, or a way to make my accusations stick.

Fourteen

I was wound up. As I lay silently in the darkness, so as not to wake up Ponpon, I made plans. There were any number of things I had to find out.

The coroner's report sent by Selçuk could shed some light on the deaths of Gül and Ceren. I could also get access to the police files on the deaths of Musa in Antalya and Muhammet in Van.

Jihad2000 could surprise me by coming up with something.

Cengiz had told me that his summer house was right next to that of the Yıldız family. That could provide some sort of lead. Even the most insignificant event or tiniest detail could prove vital.

I had to learn where Adem Yıldız was at the time of the deaths. And did the flat in Ataköy with the red star on the doorbell belong to him?

Had Adem Yıldız gone home with any of the girls the night he came to the club? If he had, with whom? I could find this out from Hasan.

I tossed and turned until dawn.

When it was time for ordinary people to start work, I ignored Ponpon's need for beauty sleep and began making phone calls. First I called Selçuk. The police are supposed to start work first thing in the morning, after all. There was no need to raise Selcuk's suspicions without proof of some kind. I didn't mention Adem Yıldız, just brought up the deaths in Van and Antalya and the disappearance of Funda, the girl working the motorway. I told him I'd need some information.

He paused for a moment.

"Look," he said. "I'll do what I can, but I can't help wondering what the guys in the department will think if I start poking my nose into a bunch of transvestite incidents that have nothing to do with us."

"I understand," I told him.

He was right. If a police chief suddenly took it upon himself to look into a case that was none of his business it would mean he was invading someone else's turf. And the transvestite angle would be enough to get tongues wagging.

"This is really getting to me," I said. "I can't get it out of my head. There's some connection between the names of the victims. I've got to find it, whatever it is."

"I see what you're getting at," he said. "But believe me, I can't promise anything. Over time, we can investigate each case. But to suddenly open all the files..."

"I see..."

"Sorry," he continued. "It's bad enough already. There's always trouble if someone's toes get stepped on."

"What do you mean, 'sorry'," I said. "There's nothing to apologise for..."

"The coroner's report came in. I had a look. There didn't seem to be anything important. Someone will bring it over to you in a bit."

"Thanks."

Something came to mind just as I was about to hang up.

"Just one more thing," I said. I mentioned the address in Ata-köy. "Could we find out who owns the flat and who's using it?"

"It's as good as done."

I thanked him again.

Would it make any sense for me to travel to Van, in the east, Antalya, down south, and Rize, all the way up on the Black Sea? Even if I went to them all, would it make a bit of difference?

Despite the early hour, I called Hasan. The phone rang repeatedly before he finally picked up, cursing under his breath.

"I know it's a bit early, but I haven't been able to sleep. I was wondering about something. Who went off with Adem Yıldız when he came to the club the other night?"

Hasan was still sleepy, and it took him some time to understand what I was getting at. I repeated my question.

"I don't know," he said. "I can't remember. There were a lot of them at the table. Ahmet Kuyu and the others. Girls were coming and going all night. A bunch went off together. They left a big tip, but I can't remember who went with them."

"You've got to find out," I said. "I need to know which of the girls left with them.'

"I'll find out. But I'm afraid there was more than one girl. There was a whole group of them together."

"All right," I said. "Find out as quick as you can who they were."

"Good morning," Ponpon sang out from her room.

"*Ayol*, what's going on in there? Even the earliest bird hasn't found the worm yet. What's the commotion?"

She came in wearing a kimono; pinkies cocked, she modestly held the front closed. It was black, and every inch was covered with embroidery. She raised her eyebrows as she spoke. On her feet were Japanese slippers. The nails of her enormous feet were painted a pale pink.

Taking tiny steps, she came over and kissed me. Then she sat down opposite. She carefully draped the kimono around her legs. Slowly, ever so slowly, she crossed them. Then she fussed once more with her kimono.

"What about my coffee?"

My unwanted guest wanted service as well.

I went to the kitchen to top up my coffee and prepare hers. I'd already had far too much of the stuff. I'd begun drinking before sunrise. In a single morning, I'd drunk more than I usually consume in a week.

"So what have you found out?" her voice floated out.

"I'm coming," I said.

"You left me all alone last night."

"You were asleep."

"So what," she protested. "Why do you think I came here in the first place? Because I was afraid of being alone. And what did you do? You went off and left me."

"Would you like milk in your coffee?"

"Please...But not too much. Two drops or so. And two sugars!"

She'd added the last bit because she knows I don't take sugar. I always forget to add sugar for my guests.

I started talking about this and that, not going into detail because I know how panicky Ponpon can be. She'd get scared while I was out.

"You're really exaggerating," she said. "Sweetie, we're all named after holy men. I mean, all right, there are some with new, modern, made-up names. But for God's sake, how many?

Generally only the young ones. Which doesn't apply to us. And there are some with Central Asian Turkic names. That's it."

There was no trace of the Ponpon who only the previous night had been fearing for her life.

"So?" I said.

"What I mean to say, sweetie, is if you dig deep enough we've all got suspect names."

I was thrilled to see her so nonplussed, and hoped it would last.

We'd sipped about half our coffee when the doorbell rang. A well-built policeman stood in the doorway, his motorcycle helmet under his arm and a large yellow envelope in his hand.

"Commissioner Selcuk Taylanc sent this," he informed me.

As I took the envelope I examined him from head to toe.

I ignored Ponpon's cry of "Who is it?"

I have a weakness for these black leather motorcycle outfits. And it's a fact that the best-looking policemen are selected for special services. They are in a completely different league from the ones responsible for traffic infractions and passport checks.

It seemed pointless to get horny at this time of day, with so much to do and Ponpon sitting inside. In any case, the boy didn't seem interested. I thanked him and closed the door.

Ponpon was even more curious than me. She grabbed one of the dossiers. We sat across from each other, reading. Apart from her asking me the meaning of every medical term she encountered, and her tiny shrieks of horror when I answered, we read the reports right through to the end.

Both of the corpses exhibited evidence of sodomy. There were no more details about Ceren, whose body had been badly burned. But her internal organs were apparently undamaged.

Traces of blood and sperm, damaged by heat, were found in her anus. What a surprise! The report was unable to determine exactly how long Gül had remained in the water. Despite the extensive swelling, the police had identified signs of trauma to her body. Her anus exhibited signs of forced entry. No traces of drugs or medication were found in her blood.

The contents of their stomachs had been analysed and the report contained details of what they had eaten, and when. There were detailed descriptions of their skin, eyes, hair and other physical characteristics. Excessive doses of oestrogen were found in Ceren's body. Despite its charred state, "deformations" had been detected in her chest and buttocks.

I read the reports stony-faced, but I was badly shaken. So was Ponpon. We avoided eye contact.

"But this is just too nauseating," she cried. "I woke up hungry for breakfast. Now I've lost my appetite."

"You said it." I agreed. "Me too."

I left Ponpon in front of the television and got on the internet. It was time to look up Jihad2000.

It didn't take long to find him. I summarised everything. I explained about Musa, Muhammet and Yunus-Funda. He was sorry he didn't know anything about them. He said he'd found out what he could.

I also asked him to investigate "adam-star", "starman" and "*adam". I just had too much to do, and he was in front of the computer all day anyway. Not only would it be a lot easier for him, it would save me a lot of time.

He asked when I would visit again. I told him I was busy these days, and that I wouldn't be able to commit myself until I'd settled everything.

I hesitated to provide him with the name Adem Yıldız. Then I decided to. After all, there was no point in my getting mixed up with that filth unless I really had to.

Fifteen

From what Hasan was able to piece together, Adem Yıldız and Ahmet Kuyu had left the club accompanied by Aylin, Vuslat and Demet.

I wanted to arrange an interview with all three girls. I could have handled things on the phone, but thought it best to meet face-to-face. It would also give me a chance to escape Ponpon's morning rituals. While I appreciate the importance of a thorough skin maintenance regime, Ponpon had embraced a daily ceremony the likes of which I'd never once encountered, whether in real life, books or film. It involved the application of every kind of cosmetic and natural preparation imaginable, in ways that aren't so easy to imagine.

I left as she began pulverizing parsley in the blender for her morning mask.

As I made my way to Aylin's house in the Cirağan district of Beşiktaş, something occurred to me. Would it be possible to analyse the sperm found on the bodies, even though they had been damaged in the fire and water? If there really were traces of sperm in the anuses of Gül and Ceren, an obvious indication that they had had sexual intercourse just prior to their deaths, would an analysis be able to indicate who their partners were?

The answers to such questions were not in my realm of

expertise. I would have to ask someone with a background in forensics. I did know, though, that such tests became more inconclusive the later they were conducted. That hag of a lady doctor could be of use to me. But at what price!

I love this neighbourhood. Despite its location in the very heart of Istanbul, it seems to me to capture everything that makes the city special: To one side is the Bosphorus; on the other, it is bordered by an enormous park, a virtual forest; charming buildings line steep cobbled streets. Most importantly, people still greet each other with *günaydin* every morning, the corner shop owner and butcher are locals, and the overall atmosphere is one of neighbourliness.

Aylin's tiny garden apartment boasts slices of Bosphorus view from between the buildings in front of hers. She had just awoken, and hadn't yet shaken off her morning grogginess. Opening the door a crack, she poked out her nose. She was astonished to see me.

"*Merhaba* hubby," she greeted me. "Welcome..."

The girls just love referring to their clients as "hubby". Some of them find it strange that I sometimes opt for men's clothing. That's what was probably behind the matrimonial reference.

"I need to have a talk," I told her.

"Come right in, *ayol*," she said.

We sat down.

The grace and beauty of her body was truly enchanting. She rivalled anything you'd see in a *Playboy* centrefold spread. Her newly acquired breasts were rather small and pert, in contrast to the Dolly Parton model that are all the rage. Like the proud owner of any new toy or bauble, she was determined to show them off. She was topless. Below, she wore only a pair of shorts.

After a brief discussion of the weather, she sipping a can of cola, me drinking a glass of water, we finally came to the point.

"The night before last," I said, "You went off with Ahmet Kuyu and company."

"Don't even remind me," she said. "You know what he's like."

"What happened; what did the two of you get up to?" I asked.

"You know what I'm like," she said. "Once the money's been handed over I'm on for anything. There's no whining about what I will or won't do. So long as he doesn't mess up my face, he's welcome to beat me once he's paid up."

As I listened to her, I felt a knot in my stomach.

"Ahmet Kuyu is one of those. You know..."

"What do you mean?"

"*Aman!* Whenever he's got a bit of cash in his pocket there's nothing he likes more than roughing up one of the girls. The more you scream and throw yourself about the more turned on he gets. I've got the guy sussed..."

As she spoke, she toyed with her breasts. She cupped them, pushed them up from below to make them stick out further, circled her nipple with an index finger and all the while gazed down at them, entranced. Needless to say, she contorted her lips into a series of expressions designed to complement the gymnastics of her breasts.

"Actually, what they really expect is for you to play along with them," she said. "I'm good. I scream to high heaven, throw myself at their feet, beg and plead... He was really taken with me. But it was the other idiot who paid the bill."

"Which one?"

"Not Adem Yıldız, the other one. You know, the one dressed like some kind of accountant."

So she knew full well who Adem Yıldız was. He hadn't even bothered to keep his identity secret.

"So what did Adem Yıldız do?" I asked.

"What do I know, *abla*? He wasn't what you'd call chatty. He just sat there, asking everyone what their name was."

So it's true he had a thing for names.

"What's your real name?" I asked.

"Seçkin," she said. "My name is proof I'm queer. My brothers were named Mustafa and Reşat, after our grand-fathers, but by the time they got to me there weren't any grandfathers left, so I was called Seçkin. It was a fashionable name at the time. When my dad found out I was queer he said, 'Just look what that name did to him!'"

Now she ran the cola can down between her breasts, trying to hold up the empty can with them. It slipped down to her lap.

"Were you with Adem Yıldız?"

"No way, *ayol*," she said. "He's a chicken hawk. I guess I was a bit too mature for him. But I still think he's the one who paid me. Where would Ahmet Kuyu get his hands on so many dollars?"

She cursed the can as it slipped off her lap and dropped to the floor.

"Did they pay in dollars?"

"Naturally... They're special customers with special tastes. The payment's got to be special too, don't you think?"

"You have a point," I agreed.

"So *abla*, what's come out of all of this? Now that I've answered your questions what have you solved?"

I laughed.

"Actually, not a thing."

"Oh...You mean to tell me I've told you all this for nothing?" she asked.

"No, not at all. It'll come in handy one day."

"Good," she said, and resumed playing with the cola can.

"What did the other girls do that night?" I asked.

"I've got no idea."

She was concentrating on her breasts again, playing with her nipples.

"They're real beauties, aren't they?"

"They're incredible," I complimented her.

"I'm just crazy about them. I could spend the whole day admiring them and still not get my fill."

"You'll get used to them," I said.

"Of course," she said, suddenly contrary. "Of course I will. It's not as though I could spend the rest of my life worshipping my tits, is it? I'm playing with them a lot now so the novelty will wear off quicker."

"Who slept with whom that night?" I asked.

"I think Adem Yıldız was with Dolly Vuslat. I told you he was a chicken hawk."

"Do you know what they did?"

"Ay, of course not," she said. "How am I supposed to know? I left as soon as I was done. I'm not one for spending the night and all that. The girls were still there...I didn't actually see them. But I'm pretty sure they were there."

"Didn't you talk to them later?"

"What about? What have I got in common with them?"

Rising to her feet, she squeezed her breasts together, then suddenly released them. They shook violently. And she was approaching me.

"Demet doesn't even bother to wax. And Vuslat's nothing but a hairy little monkey. But as for me, well, I've got breasts!"

A new caste system was emerging in the world of transvestites. Those with breasts considered themselves superior to those without. In other words, the girls with tits had decided to look down on the likes of me.

"But I haven't got any…" I began.

She interrupted. "Yes, but hubby, you're practically the boss."

The "hubby" she referred to was of course yours truly. I had no intention, and indeed would never have the intention, of playing husband to anyone, let alone one of the girls. Years earlier, out of curiosity, I had taken on the role a few times. To tell the truth, though, I don't get much pleasure out of playing husband to either men or women. At a pinch, I can do my bit, provided it is reciprocal. But there are times when, in the line of duty, as a nod to my sense of professionalism, I do what is asked of me.

Clearly, our conversation had run its course. From here on in, I could expect only that peculiar brand of silliness that I put down to excessive injections of female hormones.

When I stepped outside I noticed the air had cooled. The east wind helped clear my head. A breeze blowing in from the shores of Uskudar contained all the scents and odours of the Bosporus. The occasional whiff of exhaust fumes and petrol is Istanbul's way of flirting.

Dolly Vuslat and Demet were next in line. As I walked down the cobbled hill I realised I was hungry. It would be good to get something to eat before visiting Vuslat in Gayrettepe. What's more, dropping in on her a bit later would mean not waking her up.

I decided to go to a restaurant located on the top floor of La Maison. It has an incredible view. As I remembered their soufflés my mouth watered and my stomach growled.

It was still a bit early for lunch, so the restaurant was empty. I was the only customer. Although late in the season, the terrace was open. Not fully trusting the changeable Bosphorus breezes, I headed for a sunny table inside. The view was every bit as spectacular as I'd remembered! I'd taken to really looking at the Bosphorus the last few days. There's nothing like it during these crisp autumn days, when you feel as though you can see forever. I looked at the Maiden's Tower, Topkapı Palace, the Sublime Porte of Sarayburnu and the Sepetçiler Kasrı, letting my eyes wander up to the silhouetted minarets jutting into the sky from Haghia Sophia and the Blue Mosque. Istanbul was living up to its reputation as "the city of 1001 nights". I realised I was smiling to myself.

There were three waiters. And I was there on my own! Naturally, all eyes were on me. That is, when they weren't busy serving me they looked me over. They watched my every move. At the slightest gesture, one of them would appear at my table. I, of course, exchanged my smile for a more serious expression. It wouldn't do to be misunderstood.

The young one was just too young for me. He was a mere child. His face still bore marks of adolescence. His hands were enormous, and all out of proportion to his body. He simply would not do. From the opposite side of the terrace he raked me over with his eyes. His expression revealed nothing about his reaction to what he saw. If anything, he seemed merely curious. As though he had stumbled across a rare animal at the zoo.

The second waiter was definitely approaching his thirties and tall, but terribly ugly. In the name of professionalism, he kept his distance, but he was definitely observing me carefully.

The head waiter was middle-aged. And squat. His attentiveness bordered on harassment. It was unthinkable for me to feel any interest in him as a man. He would be well-advised to wipe completely from his mind any hopes he was entertaining.

They were as polite as can be. But observed solely with the eye of someone checking out the wares, there wasn't the slightest trace of kismet for me. I banished all lingering signs of coquetry and flirtatiousness, and ordered like a gentleman.

The chef, who I believe is French, sent out the most divine dishes from the kitchen. The chicken vol au vent was a tour de force. The celeriac salad retained its fresh colour and wasn't the least bit watery. The chocolate soufflé, which I had pre-ordered the moment I arrived, was, in a word, divine. I let each morsel slowly melt away in my mouth. Some of life's pleasures, particularly those like chocolate soufflé, should be drawn out as long as possible. In short, I was captivated by both the meal and the view.

I graciously refused their offer of coffee. The middle-aged, jaded waiter had apparently got my number. Clearly entertaining false hopes, he began hovering over me.

"Compliments of the house..." he said. Alas, it was not to be! I explained that I was in rather a hurry, and requested the bill. He pulled out my chair as I rose to my feet, and accompanied me all the way to the elevator with effusive cries of "Do come again".

Sixteen

The heavy meal and autumn sun beating in through the windows had made me feel groggy. I was ready to fall asleep. If I'd been anywhere near a bed I would have lain down. Perhaps I shouldn't have refused the complimentary coffee after all.

I was in luck. A taxi appeared immediately and I set off for Gayrettepe.

Dolly Vuslat lives on Ortaklar Caddesi in one of the few remaining apartments that isn't now used as office space.

A few months back I'd dropped in for a birthday party.

"It's really far more ... convenient ... living in a building full of offices," she'd assured me. "It's more ... comfortable. No one pokes their nose into your business. There's none of that ... needless neighbourly nonsense and snooping."

As far as I recalled, she wasn't really that young, but the Almighty had blessed her with the appearance of an eighteen-year-old. That's why she'd been known for years as Bebek, or Doll. She was still asked for ID when she visited some bars or clubs for the first time.

Dolly Vuslat was living confirmation of the old Turkish saying "A dwarf hen remains a young chicken forever", meaning "A petite woman never grows old". Her frame was tiny for a woman, let alone a man, and under the club spotlights she resembled nothing so much as a painted infant in an evening gown.

The face that greeted me at the door was devoid of makeup, and not at all doll-like. It was bruised and battered.

I went in.

"Just look at what happened to me," she began.

She wore a faded track suit, and on her feet were high-heeled lamé slippers.

"I went off with that bastard Adem Yıldız... Just look at me!"

"What happened?" I asked.

"I couldn't get it up. On account of the medication. He was furious."

"I don't understand..."

"He's a bottom. It's not my thing. You know me. Even if I were in bed with Marilyn Monroe I'd stick my rump up in the air... It just didn't happen... And he was furious..."

"Wow!" I exclaimed. "There's more to our Adem Bey than meets the eye."

"For the love of God. There are all sorts of perverts. These days there seems to be a real run on this particular kind. We're meant to do it to them. I mean, really! If that's what you're into why not go give it up to a real man. What business is it of mine, fucking some guy?" She held in her hand an old compact mirror. While talking, she examined her face. Her upper left lip was split open. As she spoke, her mouth slid sideways.

"Just look at me! It'll be at least ten days before I'm at all presentable."

I offered my condolences.

"But I do have to hand it to him. He's a big tipper. With that kind of money, I can afford not to work for a whole month, let alone ten days."

I don't get it. She'd been smacked, her face was covered with lumps, her lip split open, and she still considered it trade in kind.

"What's your real name, Vuslat?"

"That's funny. He asked the same thing. 'Haven't you got another name, a middle name or something?'"

She'd told me everything I needed to know except her name.

"Guess," she said.

It was highly unlikely I'd come up with the right name, just like that.

"How am I supposed to know? Just tell me."

"Dursun!" she laughed. "Can you imagine me with a name like Dursun?"

The phone rang. Interrupting further elaboration of the inappropriateness of her name.

"*Efendim...*" she answered. She spoke with the nasal whine adopted by so many of the girls. Even though her voice was high enough in any case.

As Vuslat conversed with a series of 'uh huh's and 'yes'es, I glanced around the room. On the wall hung a huge poster of Tom Cruise. The poor poster was plastered with sequins and a pair of false eyelashes had been glued on. Tom Cruise's once sober white shirt was a riot of glitter. Sparkles and phosphorus pens had been used to apply highly exaggerated makeup to his face. The holes in his ears were no doubt used as holders for various sets of earrings.

Vuslat ended the call with a drawn-out "No way".

"It's quite amazing, isn't it?"

She was referring to the poster.

"I did it myself."

When our girls aren't working, their range of activities are rather limited. Most, if not all, are bored by the mere thought of reading a book. They can't sit still long enough to watch a movie from start from finish. Meals are prepared with an eye to speed and convenience. The entire afternoon is spent applying makeup, styling and dyeing hair, and other creative nonsense.

As if covering their dresses and T-shirts with sequins and glitter wasn't enough, they'd moved on to defenceless Tom Cruise.

"What else did he do to you?" I asked.

"He's a real maniac, *abla*!" she said. "First he asked if I'd done my ritual ablutions. I hadn't of course, but told him otherwise. Then he went off to perform his. He washed himself from head to toe. Then prayed. While reciting "*bismillahir-rahmanirrahim*" he took mine into his mouth."

I was intrigued. I'd never come across anything like this. The most extreme case I'd encountered was Jihad2000 Kemal. However, he'd completely forgotten all about his prayers once he was erect.

"It was all I could do to get it back out of his mouth. He was so determined to finish things off that he just sucked and licked, grabbed and squeezed...If it ain't gonna happen, it ain't gonna happen!"

"Did he do anything else?" I asked.

"He sure did, *ayol*! Do you think he paid me for nothing? First he beat me up for not getting it up. It hurt like hell. Then he forced himself on me. Anyway, he's got a tiny one. It's obvious what his problem is."

She waved her pinkie in order to give me an approximate idea of the size of Adem Yıldız's penis.

"They see they're stuck with little dicks, so they hanker after a big one. But they're not considered queer. We are."

She narrowed her eyes and leaned towards me, as though she were preparing to share a secret.

"You know what," she said. "Even if I'd done it to him I'd still be called an *ibne*. What's the difference? I just don't get it!"

She had a point. I didn't understand either.

"He called me later. 'Let's try again' he said."

"Was that him on the phone?" I asked.

"No way, *ayol*!" It was the corner store. The owner's son. He swings by sometimes; I get behind on my account. He asks if I've run out of anything, then offers to come by with some milk or sugar."

"You've got plenty of money There's no need for any of that," I said.

"Don't you get it?" she corrected me. "The boy is so handsome! Exactly my type. He just finished his military service. Those bulging muscles, that chest like a hairy jungle. And his arms...now, that's what I call a man! He's got my number, no doubt about it. But I don't want him to see me like this. After the swelling goes down a bit."

"I see," I said.

"In any case," she added. "The wait will make him even hornier."

I wasn't too interested in the sexy son of the market owner.

"What was Adem Yıldız's home like?" I asked

"I've got no idea. We didn't go there. We went to Ahmet

Kuyu's house. It's on the other side. In a garden. It was dark so I don't even know exactly where it is."

"In Göksu," I remembered.

I knew the house. I'd passed by once. Ahmet Kuyu had given me a try too, just as he had everyone else. But he'd regretted it. He'd apologised later and even helped me out with some work-related business of mine. Since that time, we'd only ever exchanged formal greetings when we ran into each other.

"Whatever, that's the place," Vuslat said. "He didn't take me to his own house."

"How are you going to call him?" I asked.

"There's no need," she replied. "He calls me every day."

Dolly Vuslat needed a warning. If he was really phoning her every day, she could find herself in big trouble. But how much should I tell her? All of my suspicions? If it turned out that she trusted him more than me, or considered the whole thing a joke, or just wanted to get more money, she could well spill the beans, pass along everything I'd told her. Then I'd be the one in big trouble. If Adem Yıldız sent his men after me how many would I be able to fight off?

While I was weighing this up, my eyes strayed to the Tom Cruise poster. Could I really trust someone with such a kitsch approach to life?

On the other hand, I imagined the pangs of conscience I'd suffer if something terrible happened to the girl.

My concerns about my conscience won out, and I decided to tell her, omitting as many details as possible. She sat hunched on the sofa, knees pulled up to her chin, emitting periodic short, sharp screams until I was finished. Her hands, bunched up in fists, were pressed to her lips and her eyes wide open with fear.

"That's about it," I concluded.

"My God, I'm terrified," she said. "I knew the guy wasn't normal but . . . a serial killer!"

"Look, I told you all of this so you'd be careful. Not to frighten you. As I said, we don't know anything for sure. But whatever you do, be careful."

Laughing, she walked me to the door.

"Would you believe it? This is the first time the name Dursun has done me any good. What if I'd been named İsa, Musa, Nuh, Hazreti Ali, Hasan, Hüseyin or something like that! I might be dead."

I didn't mention the fact that Hazreti Ali wasn't really a prophet, that he was the uncle of the Prophet, and Ali's sons were Hasan and Hüseyin. I just left it. She could continue reeling off the names of prophets to herself.

What I'd learned was enough. That is, Adem Yıldız occasionally surrendered himself to our well-endowed sweeties.

Seventeen

Actually, I'd found out all I wanted to know. There was no need to pay a call on Demet. What's more, when I thought about how out of the way her house was it put me off the idea even more.

Cengiz could wait. There was no way Adem Yıldız would have had his fun at his family's summer house, risking his reputation. In any case, I had other reasons to see Cengiz. Something more might develop between us.

I was eager to get back home as soon as possible to look over any new information sent by Selçuk and to find out what else Jihad2000 had been able to learn.

Although it's not my habit, I decided to get on the metro, since I was so close to a stop. It was better than getting stuck in traffic, fending off the meaningless prattle of a taxi driver or having to listen to his choice of music on the radio. Furthermore, it would be the fastest way to get home.

Billboards displayed the *börek* and pastries sold by the Yıldız market chain. They bragged that the number of stores had doubled in just five years, talked of embracing consumers of all ages and thanked Turkey for its appreciation of Yıldız products.

It was a vivid reminder of Adem Yıldız, and an omen of the darkest kind.

I couldn't wait to tell someone that Adem Yıldız was the passive partner in bed. But who? I felt like I'd explode if I couldn't share this juicy nugget with someone. Whether or not he was the killer, he was certainly a pillar of society. And he gave it up in bed. And to whom!

Ponpon came to mind first. I doubted I'd get satisfaction from her, though. She always went one better. If I mentioned having a headache, she'd double over with cramps. If I brought up Adem Yıldız, she'd be sure to reel off a list of famous men of the same persuasion. I mean, what's the point of a good gossip with someone like that?

It was a short walk from the Taksim metro stop to my home. There was a chill in the air, and the slope to Gümüşsuyu was windy as usual, winter and summer.

Hasan seemed the most worthy of my news. He'd be on the phone to someone else before it even had a chance to sink in.

The general upheaval, open window and freezing cold that greeted me as I entered my house were all signs that Satı had come. I'd completely forgotten that it was her day to clean.

Under Ponpon's supervision she had taken up all the carpets, stacked the chairs onto each other and pulled out the heavy furniture. Muttering under her breath, Satı cleaned in a distant corner. I could read displeasure on her face. If this went on, and Ponpon stayed for another ten days, I was liable to lose Satı.

Dressed for cleaning, Ponpon had wrapped her head in a gypsy-pink turban, Maharajah style.

"Welcome home, sweetie," she sang out. "I thought I'd best get this house sorted. I may as well be of some use while I'm here."

"Madame had me pull everything out."

Sati sounded utterly defeated. "Madame" obviously referred to Ponpon.

I wasn't expecting this at all. Ponpon's known for her tidiness, but she was now imposing her idea of orderliness on me. It would be impossible for me to get any work done or to collect my thoughts. I felt like fleeing on the spot.

"Er, well done," I said. "Keep up the good work. Have you got much more to do?'

"We've only just started. Satı Hanım didn't even get here until nearly 11:00."

"But you asked me not to come early," said Satı, defensively.

"We hoovered all the curtains. They were black with dust! It's not obvious at night, but in the morning light I just couldn't believe my eyes. Satı Hanım, dear, could I ask you to wash them all at least once a month? The longer you let things go the worse it gets."

Ponpon had taken over. There was no point in saying anything. I wouldn't be able to get a thing done with the house in this state. I went into my study and shut the door.

I called Hasan the minute I sat down. As always, the line was busy. He'd die if he knew what he was missing. Eh, there's such a thing as fate.

Next I called Selçuk. He wasn't there. I was told he'd be back shortly. The secretary was a capable girl.

"Have you received the envelope we sent you?" she asked, underlining her authority and proving she knew who I was.

"If you'd prefer, we'll get back to you," she added. "Where can we reach you?"

"That'd be great," I said. "I'm at home."

Under these conditions, with my home sweet home turned

upside down, however, I wasn't certain how much longer I would be able to stay. But for the moment anyway, home I was.

My computer had warmed up, and I got online. Something told me not to contact Jihad2000 just yet. I'd followed my hunches so far, and this was no time to abandon them.

While waiting for Selçuk's call I did a little research into the Yıldız markets. They had their own website, of course. They even offered home delivery to some parts of town. On one of the "corporate background" pages appeared a photograph of the family patriarch. He was clean shaven, without a trace of a beard or moustache, and had the intense gaze of one who has put his trust entire and solely in God. He looked exactly like a self-assured candidate forwarded by a conservative political party.

Father Yıldız related how "by the grace of God" they achieved such success and how his "faith" had always helped show him the way.

Adem Yıldız was pictured on a page devoted to the corporate executives. He displayed a bashful smile, with just a hint of teeth showing between thin lips. I'd read in *Radikal* newspaper that the children of religious families were invariably educated in America. I wondered once again why they weren't sent to countries like Iran, Afghanistan, Saudi Arabia or at least Egypt.

The products page was mouth-watering. Despite the lingering flavour of soufflé on my palate, the pastries pictured had me salivating.

The company has branches in virtually all of Turkey's provinces, with 16 outlets in Istanbul alone. I discovered that there was one shop in Van and three in Antalya. What did that mean? Adem Yıldız could have paid a visit to either city. Then

again, there were plenty of reasons to visit Antalya other than
family business.

I was just beginning to lose interest when the phone rang.

The all-knowing secretary was on the other end.

"I'll put you through to the chief," she said.

A moment later, I was on the phone with Selçuk.

"*Merhaba* Poirot."

"You may refer to me as Miss Marple," I shot back. "I'm
dying of curiosity."

"First," he began, "the address you asked about is owned by
Fehmi Şenyürek, and the records show that he also resides
there." Strike one. The red-star flat didn't belong to Adem
Yıldız, as I'd supposed.

"What's wrong?" Selçuk asked.

"Nothing," I replied. "It's just that the name doesn't mean
anything to me. I was thinking."

"There's nothing to think about. I did some digging for
you."

"Who is he?"

"He was born in Gemlik in 1967. Expelled from military
college. Right now he's employed by a private sector company.
He received a direct loan from Emlakbank to buy his flat."

"Were you able to learn which company he works for?"

"We can check that out from other sources."

"If it's not too much trouble, would you mind?"

"We'll try," he promised.

"And the other things?" I prompted.

"One at a time," he said.

"All right. But I've got one last question. A DNA test wasn't
conducted on the sperm found in the anuses of Ibrahim

Karaman and Yusuf Seçkin. Could one be done?"

"So much time has passed. I'm really not sure."

"Well," I said, "I was thinking that a sperm analysis could identify their sexual partners."

"You might be right," he said. "Hold on a minute. Just let me ask."

I was put on hold. Ponpon poked her head through the door. "Good for you, *ayol*," she said. "I was listening outside."

"You've got no shame!" I scolded her.

"*Aman.* I thought the call might be for me, but you beat me to it. Then I heard what you were talking about. Well, I couldn't hang up, could I? So I listened for a bit. What's the big deal?"

There's just no point in trying to explain some things to Ponpon. The way she'd pillaged and plundered my house demonstrated her sense of boundaries. According to her, anything goes when it comes to friends.

Selçuk was back on the line.

"You'll never guess what I found out," he said. "It's possible to analyse sperm found in the vagina or anus of a corpse – even if it's been in water for three days. Seawater or freshwater, makes no difference. If the sperm's in the body's mouth, though, forget it. But in the anus or vagina, no problem."

"So why didn't they do a test?"

"That's what I was wondering."

We were both silent.

Ponpon was standing right next to me. Unable to hear what was being said, she looked at me curiously.

"What happened?" she whispered.

I covered the receiver with my hand. "I'll tell you later."

Shaking her head, she assumed a knowing look and bit her lower lip.

"Selçuk," I said, "Is there any way we could get those tests done?"

"What do you mean 'we', pal?"

"Excuse me," I said. "What I meant was, could you have it done?"

"I'll try," he said. "I'll see what I can do. The boys get down to work if you push them a bit. They must have been too busy to bother. As far as I know, the tests are pretty complicated. And pricey. It'll take some time, too."

"I'll pay whatever is necessary," I said.

"Don't be silly. Look, I've got to run. I hope you don't mind my hanging up on you like this."

"What do you mean? Not at all."

"Don't forget," he ended. "Ayla and I are expecting you. Don't leave it too long."

"Sure," I told him.

Ponpon pounced the second I hung up the phone. She peppered me with questions.

I told her what I'd learned. She responded to everything I said with a fascinated "Oh, you don't say." But when I finished, she pushed me over the edge by declaring, "So what's the big deal?"

She had a point.

Other than speculation and suspicions, we had nothing to go on.

"Come on," she said. "I made some *dolma*. Stuffed peppers and tomatoes. You'll love them."

"I ate out."

"You're crazy, *ayol*," she nagged. "I mean, everyone knows what a great cook I am. Yet you go off to some restaurant. Shame on you!"

Trying to get anything done at home was proving to be extremely taxing. The best thing would be to go and shut myself up in my office. I'd have to deal with Ali, the messages I'd failed to answer, business developments, sector chatter and dozens of annoying requests for my assistance, but I'd still be better off far away from Ponpon and Satı.

Eighteen

I put on a thick jacket as a precaution against the cooling weather, and headed out to the street. I was exhausted. What with the racket of the washing machine, vacuum cleaner and Ponpon's shrieked commands, I'd forgotten to call a taxi. I walked to the stand.

Hüseyin works nights, so wasn't available. That was just as well. I was in no mood to cope with his flirting. I got into the first taxi waiting at the stand. I couldn't decide between going to the office and paying a visit to Jihad2000 Kemal. I decided to give Kemal some more time to finish his research.

The office workers all respect me immensely. They just find me a bit odd. I'm fully aware that they describe me using terms like "interesting", "eccentric" and "unconventional". While they're generally accustomed to seeing me dressed as a man, I have been known on occasion to arrive with a two-day beard, full eye makeup, rouge and lipstick just to shock annoying clients.

Ali was out. For the moment, that was just as well. There was no one there to drag me into conversation.

Clearing a workspace, I pushed aside the pile of mail left on my desk by the secretary.

Now, everything was ready – except me. I didn't know where to start. All right, I was going to get to work. But on what? Where should I begin, and where would it lead?

I was convinced of Adem Yıldız's guilt. That much was certain. But there wasn't a shred of evidence to implicate him. He was a piece of filth, a real pervert. So what did that prove? And that was the problem in a nutshell.

I had plenty of time. I decided to check through the chat room records. Even though I had no idea what I was looking for, I would scan the entries made by "adam star", "starman" and "*adam".

"You have a call, sir. I'm putting you through."

The secretary needed a good dressmg down. By simply announcing that a call was being put through, the assumption was that I was compelled to accept it.

"What's up, *abla*?"

It couldn't be, but it was. Yes, it was on Gönül on the line. I'd completely forgotten that I'd ever given her my number.

"*Merhaba* Gönül," was my forced greeting.

"Ay! So you know who it is."

"Why wouldn't I? How could I ever forget you?"

"You really mean that, don't you?"

"What is it, anyway? I'm busy. I'm working," I said.

I just left the coroner's. I thought I'd fill you in."

I'd forgotten all about that, too.

"Any leads?" I asked.

"Oh, it hurt like hell. Had I known, I swear I'd never have agreed. That fiendish witch of a woman. Just like that, she shoved a whole length of icy iron right up my arse."

I wouldn't require details. I could easily imagine what her "voluntary" examination had been like. What's more, it didn't answer my question.

"What about Gül's death?" I prompted her. "Any leads or developments?"

"You bet!" she exclaimed. And was silent.

"What?"

"Look *abla*, It's too long to go into on the phone. And you're busy. I don't want to take your precious time. I'll tell you everything next time we meet."

And she hung up.

If she'd been within arm's reach, I'd have strangled her.

To make matters worse, I had no idea how to find her. I guessed she was a regular at the rough beer houses of Aksaray. Or worse. But I didn't know where she lived or spent her time. The only place I was certain to find her was at the coroner's or at a funeral. Perhaps I wouldn't see her again until another girl died.

My only hope was that she'd call me.

Unbalanced people and unhinged situations tend to throw my equilibrium out of whack as well. With no idea what to do, I sat staring at the wall opposite.

Ali's arrival ended that little reverie.

That secretary would have to be disciplined. She was supposed to check with me first, then connect my calls.

"I've got great news for you!" be announced. Remember that Italian company, Mare T.Docile? It's as good as done. I think I've landed a deal. Time for the money to roll in..."

He rubbed his hands together with glee. A grin stretched from ear to ear. As usual, when talking about money his eyes narrow to slits and his face seems to glow with a strange lust.

My thoughts were elsewhere. Talk of Italians and their lire would have no effect on me.

"Hey, what's up?" he asked. "We've been chasing after this

account for two months. Now we've got it. You're not even reacting. What's wrong with you?"

"Don't mind me," I said. "I was thinking about something else."

"There'll be none of that. You've got to concentrate. This is our biggest account ever. We've got to focus on it from now on. We could even retire if we handle it right. Just think about the money we'll make!"

"How much is it?" I asked.

The figure he cited was roughly the equivalent of winning the national lottery.

"They want to have a meeting with the two of us as soon as possible. We may even need to go to their headquarters in Geneva or offices in Nice to inspect their networks."

He knows how much I hate business travel.

"It won't take long. Just a few days. And we can spend a couple of them having fun. Shopping and stuff..."

"I can handle everything right here," I reminded him. "Advanced technology makes that possible."

"I know that. It's just not what they want. They tell me their main systems are closed to outside intervention. They're unique and they have their own software program. The customer's always right."

"Ali," I said sharply. "We've been working together all these years. How many times do I have to tell you that the system they use and the protective shield are completely independent of each other."

"I know," he allowed. "But..."

"No 'but's' about it. If I can't get this through your head I don't see how I'm supposed to explain it to them."

"Now don't go off in a tizzy."

"I'm not. Tell me again. What kind of figure are we talking about here?"

He repeated the amount.

It really would be best for me to forget everything and start thinking about what I could do with that money. My cut would be more than enough. I could buy up all the shares in the club, or even open a new one. In fact, I could open a summer club in Bodrum and use the one in Istanbul during the winter.

I let my imagination run wild: I could do my work in Berlin or Paris. Or I could give up this racket and become the star attraction of clubs all across the globe. I could visit every transvestite club and bar on the planet. Who knows the things I'd see, that I'd experience!

"We've got to get to work immediately," Ali said. "I've even brought you some files for homework."

As Ali went out to get the Mare T.Docile files I looked at the piece of paper on my desk. I'd made a list of all the dead girls. Their nicknames and male names were all in a row. In the adjacent column I'd jotted down the specifics of their deaths and noteworthy details, if any.

I began the moment Ali walked back in carrying two CD-Roms.

"You know that friend of yours, Cengiz..."

"You liked him, didn't you?" he interrupted. "I knew he'd be just your type."

"He said he had a summer house right next to Adem Yıldız's place..."

"That's right," said Ali. "A summer house in Bodrum, on Mazi harbour. But his ex-wife and kids are there right now."

"Shut up a minute," I said. "Stop interrupting me. There's something else I want to ask."

"All right...all right!"

"How well do you think he knows Adem Yıldız?"

"Did you like him too?"

"Don't be ridiculous," I said. "I've got my suspicions. I need some information. Make it hush-hush though."

"Talk to Cengiz," he said. "There's no way for me to know..."

The subject was closed and he placed the CD-Roms in front of me.

"You'll find all the system specifications and the various problems they've faced to date. I'd like you to have a look. I told them we'd be finished reviewing everything by the beginning of next week. We will be finished, won't we?"

I, too, had fallen under the spell of the expected payment from Mare T.Docile.

Nineteen

By the time I left the office it was after 8pm. Mare T.Docile's computer systems were certainly complex. In order to avoid paying tax on their shipping business the company's activities were listed as being based in Split, Croatia and some islands in the Pacific Ocean. Mare T.Docile may have officially been an Italian company, but all of their container ships were in fact leased at a near loss to these fly-by-night firms.

When I got home I was greeted by a reproachful Ponpon.

"*Ayol*, where you have you been? I've run myself ragged heating and reheating dinner. I was just about to sit down and eat alone."

My home, my sweet home, was a place of gleaming parquet floors. The furniture had all been rearranged according to Ponpon's tastes. There wasn't a trace of my calculated efforts to create a post-modern effect. I now resided in what could easily have passed for a granny flat.

As I looked over her handiwork, Ponpon smiled at me proudly.

"It's so much better now, don't you think?" she asked.

"Thanks for taking so much trouble," I replied. What else could I say?

"Satı and I worked our fingers to the bone, of course, but it was worth it. I had to follow her from corner to corner. They just don't get down to work unless you stand over them."

"Too true," I agreed.

"This Satı Hanım of yours is a bit lazy. She supposedly comes three times a week, but dust has been collecting under the carpets for months at least. I'll send you my Zerrin. Give her a try. She's a real whirlwind!"

I smiled weakly. In fact, I was close to tears.

"And now for our dinner. I made fresh okra with chicken. With lots of lemon."

The chicken okra was delicious. If Ponpon stayed long-term I was sure to put on as much weight as she had.

"Did anyone call while I was out?" I asked.

"Ah, of course! I almost forgot," she said. "That police friend of yours called. He's got news. Ferruh or Fabri, or something like that."

"What exactly was it?" I asked.

She must have been talking about Fatih Şenyürek.

"He didn't say. He's going to call you back."

"Anyone else?" I prompted.

"*Ay*, and you've got a phone pervert! I pick up, but there's no sound. I hear him breathing, but he doesn't say a word. Calls every half hour. He'll be calling in a minute. What a weirdo, don't you think?"

"And Hasan?" I asked.

"He didn't call. I called him to find out what was going on. But he didn't have anything new."

I waited for Ponpon to leave so I could call Jihad2000, who I suspected was the heavy breather, and Selçuk. She seemed determined to stay put.

"When are you going out?" I asked her hopefully.

"Oh, I'm not," she replied. "I'm off tonight. I don't have any extra business either. I thought we'd enjoy some girl talk in front of the TV. A long merciless gossip about everyone we know..."

I love chatting with Ponpon, but this wasn't the night for it. I had other things to do. Before I concentrated on getting rich with the Mare T.Docile account, I wanted to solve the prophet murders, or at least resolve some of the puzzling questions spinning through my head.

"I hope you don't mind, but I've got to get some work done," I told her.

Her face fell.

"And what am I supposed to do while you're working?

"Watch TV, or put on one of my new DVDs. I could rustle up a visitor for you if you like."

"Don't be silly, *ayol*," she said. "I gave that up long ago."

Everyone knew Ponpon was an asexual transvestite. In fact, some suggested she'd become a cross-dresser just to spite her family.

"What I'd really like is to sit at your side," she persisted. "I'll make tea or coffee. I could even pop some corn. We'll chat while you work. I promise not to bother you."

This is just great, I thought. It seemed like a joke, but Ponpon never indulges in them.

Laughing lightly, I said, "I'm afraid it wouldn't work out."

"What do you mean, it wouldn't. Of course it would," she insisted. "Go and get started and I'll bring some tea."

Hoping the preparation of the tea would keep her busy for some time, I called Selçuk. His wife Ayla answered. She said they were expecting me for dinner Saturday evening. I accepted. Then she handed the phone to Selçuk.

"You remember your man, Fehmi Şenyürek," he began. "He works for a shipping company by the name of Astro."

"I've never heard of it," I said.

"Me neither. But I did some research. It's a subsidiary company of Yıldız." Lightning struck. I heard bells.

"Not the Yıldız chain of markets?" I said, seeking confirmation.

"That's the one. He's even got a small airline. The company's growing quietly but surely."

"I really appreciate this," I thanked him.

"I don't understand what you're after, but I'm glad to turn up something for you. Oh, and the DNA tests are being done. I'll let you know the minute the results come in."

Selçuk was absolutely right when he said they were growing quietly but surely. The Yıldız Group didn't appear in the media much. I couldn't decide if that was by design, or the result of an incompetent PR department. I seemed to recall, though, that conservative companies generally prefer the stealthy approach. Not much information leaks out, but, below the radar, slowly but surely... And without attracting any attention.

I'd connected to the internet by the time Ponpon came in with the tea, and was researching Astro shipping and StarAir. Other than chamber of commerce registration records, there was next to no information.

"You know what," said Ponpon. "Whenever you concentrate on something you've got this way of pursing your lips and frowning. I've always noticed it." She contorted her face to illustrate.

"It's such a shame, *ayol*," she went on. "You'll get wrinkles. Once those lines have set in there's no getting rid of them. You've got to look after yourself. I recommend facial masks. I'll go and whip one up if you like. It dries on your face like some kind of shell. You can't wrinkle your forehead if you try. Or you could get those injections. You know, like Tansu Çiller. Or save your money and use sellotape. That stops you screwing up your face too."

"Botox," I said.

"That's it."

It wouldn't be a bad idea to dispatch Ponpon to the kitchen while I got on-line with Jihad2000. I wasn't sure what kind of messages Jihad2000 would write, and I really couldn't risk Ponpon reading them.

"What kind of mask are you going to make?" I asked.

"Well, there's nothing handier than a good mud mask. Open jar, spread on face. Presto!"

That wouldn't do. She'd be back, jar in hand, in seconds. I tried to think of something more time-consuming.

"Haven't you got anything a bit more unusual?" I suggested. "You know, all natural ingredients, Ayurvedic and the like..."

"Don't I just!" she pounced. "It's a fabulous concoction of my own. But it'll take some time to prepare. If you'll hang on for a bit I'll go and whip it up for you. But promise to wait patiently!"

I did my best to look intrigued.

"How long will it take?"

"Well, I'd say at least..." She was calculating the ingredients needed, the time to prepare each one. "It'll take a good twenty minutes, minimum."

"That's great!" I replied with genuine enthusiasm. "If you

get started right away we can wash it off before we go out to the club."

"You bet!"

Nothing makes Ponpon happier than being entrusted with a task. Buzzing with a sense of mission, she trotted off to the kitchen.

I began hunting down Jihad2000.

He is online every waking moment, and his favourite pastimes involve haranguing or proselytizing those in the chat rooms. I located him immediately. He was in our "manly-girls" room, but hadn't activated his status icon. I hate lurkers. I just don't see the point in concealing your very existence in what is already a world of "virtual" names, descriptions, desires and orgasms. He spotted me right away, and opened a private window.

<where on earth have you been
i waited all day for you
i didn't even get online>

<I was busy.>

<when are you coming>

<It's just not convenient right now.>

He immediately sent a float.

<Beware! Beware!
BISMI'LLAHI'R-RAHMANI'R-RAHIM

ALL MIGHTY LORD SPARE US FROM INFIDELS
SHOW THE TRUE PATH TO GOOD AND BAD ALIKE
SHOW THEM THE PATH OF TRUTH,
RIGHTEOUSNESS AND JUSTICE HAVE MERCY ON US!
HEY GODLESS ONES! HEY INFIDELS!
HEY UNMINDFUL SINNERS!
REPENT!
REPENT AND ESCAPE THE FLAMES OF HELL>

Clearly, this was not going to work out. He was determined to roll out any and all variations of the Koranic verses, prayers and sermons that came to mind.

<Go on like this, and I'll out you.>

I selected "99" as the number of times I wanted this message sent. He would be sure to notice. And he did.

<sorry>

His return to lower case was a good sign.

<Have you found anything out>

<a bit>

<What>

<i know better than to tell you here
and I'll know more tomorrow

come over if you really want to know>

Reciprocal blackmail had begun. If he was spoiling for a
fight, I was ready. But first I had to know what he'd found out.

<when will you come tomorrow>

<I can't really say>

<i can't keep my mother outside all day
give me a time:)>

I had to admire his persistence. But that didn't mean I had
any intention of being the plaything of a pervert. I'd rather his
mother be at home when I arrive. I could go in the morning,
but tell him I'd be arriving in the afternoon. That would more
or less guarantee the presence of his mother.

<In the afternoon>

<when
exact time>

<I don't know, after 3, ok?>

<ok
but don't be late
i'll be getting ready for you>

I could only guess at the perversions involved in "getting
ready".

<Just give me a clue
What did you find out?>

<no way
i want you here with me>

The last thing I needed was a pervert on my hands. He was
as weird as something from a B horror flick. Seeing that he had
no intention of telling me anything, there was no point in
continuing to chat. The conversation would go nowhere. At
most he'd write something racy and jerk off over it. I would
not, indeed could not, be a party to such things. Then I
thought of all the things I had been a party to, and my chat
friend's desires suddenly seemed almost tame.

Ponpon's voice sang out from inside: "I've finished off your
honey. I hope you've got some more."

"It doesn't matter," I said.

"I can't hear you," she shrieked. "What was that? I can't
hear you over the blender!"

I switched off the computer and went to the kitchen, to
Ponpon. It was time for our beauty treatment.

Twenty

The mask prepared by Ponpon had the colour and consistency of baby excrement. I hesitated to have it spread it on my face.

"First, we'll apply a skin tonic made of bijapura, I mean citrus medica and jayanti, that is to say sesbania seban," she began.

The liquid used to cleanse my skin smelled wonderful, but had a disgusting colour.

"What is this stuff?" I asked.

"*Ay*, I told you. Bijapura and jayanti. They're from India..."

"You may have told me, but I'm not sure I..."

"Never mind," she interrupted. I'm not sure exactly what they are. The important thing is, they work. I order them over the internet, and they're here courtesy of DHL in less than a week."

"Great," I said.

"Shhh! Be quiet. The mask won't set properly unless you're completely calm and serene. Don't get all irritable or it won't work."

She moved on to the muddy baby shit, and was spreading it on my face with the attention of a microsurgeon.

"No talking, *ayol*!" she scolded. I kept my mouth shut.

"If you really want to know, it's bijapura again, but this time not a diffusion, the whole thing, and it's mixed with honey. Oh, and a pinch of ground fresh walnut shell . . . That'll help exfoliate any dead cells . . . It's great for deep-down cleansing. And it helps prevent blackheads . . . "

Once she'd finishing applying the mask she stepped back and examined me critically. Yes, I was a success.

"Now there'll be no talking for at least half an hour."

She tidied up the kitchen, gathering up her things and singing. It was hard to believe that someone who had appeared on stage for so many years could have such an awful voice. I couldn't help myself. I started to laugh.

"Don't laugh, *ayol*!" she said. "It'll wreck the mask . . . Just so you know, I'm not making you another one!"

I bit the insides of my cheeks.

"Come on," she said. "Show me the new porn you downloaded from the internet. Who was that guy, the one like a Greek statue . . . Have you got anything new of his?

She was talking about John Pruitt. I'd already copied all my photos and solo films of John Pruitt onto a CD for her. As far as I knew, John Pruitt had done nothing but solos. I'd never spotted him in real porn, gay or straight.

Because I was forbidden to speak, I used sign language to tell her I didn't have anything new.

"I don't believe it!" she said. "You mean to tell me they haven't taken any more pictures or made any new films of that hunk? What a disgrace!"

We returned together to the computer. I presented her with everything I'd downloaded from the net. Her examination of the contents of each album was punctuated with cries of "I've got this one", "I just love him" and "Ugh, this one's horrible". Anything that caught her eye was transferred to a dossier I'd opened just for her. Later, we'd download them onto a CD.

There was still time before my mask came off, and I was in no mood for porn. I looked at the pictures with all the interest of someone who has just blown three loads.

I began making a new list on the empty sheet of paper lying in front of me. Ponpon actually glanced at me from the corner of her eye, before returning all her attention to the business at hand. My list started off with the male and female names of all the victims Then I wrote the name Adem Yıldız, followed by adam star, starman, *adam and red star. Next to Jihad2000, I jotted down Kemal Barutçu. Last of all, I wrote Fehmi Şenyürek.

As I glanced over the list, I reached over in front of Ponpon to get a red-ink pen. Next to "red star" I scribbled a huge red star. Ponpon checked to see what I was doing.

"How do you know that madman?"

I thought she was referring to Jihad2000. I pointed to his name with the pencil, since I was forbidden to speak.

"No, not him, *ayol*," she said, "Fehmi Şenyürek."

The mask flew out the window.

"Who is he?" I asked.

"Who do you think? Just my biggest admirer. He comes to see me perform at least once a week. He always sends flowers. He leaves huge tips. As you see, he's my number one fan."

It was just the information I was looking for, from the last person I expected to provide it.

"So he's just a club acquaintance, then?" I quizzed her.

"Not at all, *ayol*. He took to inviting me to his table and introducing me to his friends. Oh, by the way, he always runs with a big crowd. There's almost never a lady at his table. As you can guess, he's a real boy-lover, a true *oğlancı*. He's not one of those who come with women just to watch us, to make fun of us. He comes for pleasure."

I paused to collect my thoughts. I hadn't seen Ponpon perform for years, but from what I could remember she was no artist. Or a singer. Or even a comedienne. I kept my thoughts to myself. There was no point in voicing them.

"Then he started inviting me to dinner. After the show…"

"Did you go with him?"

"*Ayol*, do you think I'd just run off with a strange man? Is that what you think of me?" She gave a low laugh. "Anyway, we had fish on the Bosphorus. Just the two of us."

"You are now going to remember every single thing you said and tell me word for word."

She looked directly into my eyes, without blinking.

"I'm not sure I'll be able to tell you absolutely everything."

She paused for a full three seconds, then, clearly modelling herself on Julia Roberts, gave me a lascivious wink. Next, she attempted the famous smile. She couldn't possibly pull it off! Julia Roberts amounted to half a Ponpon. In terms of both age and weight!

"What do you mean you're not sure you can tell me?" I said. "You remember things said a dozen years ago. Word for word. And you can't recall a dinner conversation from three days ago?"

"That's not it," said Ponpon Roberts. "What passed between us was just too private. I couldn't possibly repeat it."

I hovered over her.

"Now listen, and listen good! This is no laughing matter! That man could be dangerous!"

The innocent, engaging Julia Roberts was gone, replaced by a panicked Ponpon. The scream she attempted to repress had the tone of an Yma Sumac classic, the intensity of a pressure cooker.

Lips trembling, she stared at me with eyes like saucers.

I explained. "He's one of Adem Yıldız's men. They've been working together for years. Fehmi works for him," I said. "They may have done everything together. And in any case, Adem Yıldız is bottoming for our girls. Who knows just what the two of them are capable of?"

I'd finally let the cat out of the bag, but Ponpon merely held her breath and looked at me expectantly, waiting for more. She hadn't even reacted to my news about Adem Yıldız. My bombshell had fizzled right out.

"And that admirer of yours has a flat in the building where Deniz died," I added.

This time she failed to suppress a scream.

"*Ay!* I'm terrified . . . " she screeched.

A frightened, overly excited or panicked Ponpon is a sure sign that worse is on the way. The last thing I needed was a fit of hysteria. That was definitely best avoided.

"I could be wrong," I reassured her. "I haven't got a shred of proof. I'm only acting on a hunch. That's why you've to got to tell me all you know, everything you can remember. The answer to the whole puzzle could lie in some tiny detail.

Deep in thought, Ponpon gnawed the nail of her pinkie.

"So, Fehmi *Bey*'s boss may be some crazed killer? And Fehmi is his accomplice, is that right?"

"At least that's what I suspect at the moment..." I confirmed.

I expected those words to calm her down; instead, she began trembling.

"Tell me the truth," she said. "Is he the killer? Is it Fehmi?"

"I don't know," I admitted.

And I really didn't.

I'd slapped my forehead, getting sticky baby poo all over my hand.

"I don't think so..." I backtracked. By the time I'd washed my hands and face she was weeping uncontrollably.

"Why can't I have a single normal relationship? My greatest admirer turns out to be a murderer."

"It's not him!" I sharply corrected her.

She raised her head, looking at me hopefully. Her mascara had run.

"It's not him, is it?" she half pleaded.

"I told you, I just don't know," I repeated. "He could well be the killer's henchman. Or at least mixed up in it."

"If he was some crazed killer he wouldn't have chased after me for so long, would he?" she asked herself, brightening. "I've seen it in films. People get killed right on the spot. If he was really a murderer he wouldn't go through so much trouble, spend so much money on me, would he?"

"No, he wouldn't."

I decided to drop it. Pursuing the subject would get me nowhere. And the last thing I needed was for Ponpon to fall apart.

Twenty-one

After washing her face, Ponpon joined me. Dimming the lights, she sat down opposite.

"I feel better now," she said. "Ask me anything you want."

"There's something I need to know," I said. "Just tell me, from the beginning, everything that's happened. Don't worry about the order. Any little detail could be important."

She settled into her chair, drawing on all her years on the stage as she prepared to face an audience of one: me. She cleared her throat with a tiny cough.

"I'll be back in a second," I told her, and went to the kitchen to pour myself half a glass of whiskey.

"All right, I'm ready now..." she said.

It wasn't long before I regretted having told her the order wasn't important. What she told me involved not only her entire life story, but that of everyone she had ever been involved with. James Joyce, Virginia Woolf, Marcel Proust and even Oğuz Altay would have envied her stream of consciousness narrative skills.

I thought I'd fall asleep before she ever got to the bit about Fehmi. But I didn't. I did get up and phone the club, though, to let them know I might be late, or perhaps not even show up. I was prepared to devote my entire night to Ponpon on the off chance of being provided with a critical detail.

I knew all about her past, as well as most of her adventures...I mentally filtered them out, concentrating only on Fehmi.

Fehmi Şenyürek hadn't been on the scene for all that long. At most, since the beginning of summer. And if he had ever come to watch her show before, Ponpon couldn't remember having seen him. Then, one night, just before the summer holiday, he'd arrived as part of a large group at Zilli *meyhane*, a nightclub where she regularly worked. It was probably a weeknight, since there weren't many customers. As always on nights like that, a large group attracted the attention of both the waiters and those performing on stage. They'd requested a bunch of songs from the warm-up act that went on before Ponpon, singing along with the poor girl in total disregard of tune or lyrics.

For some reason, perhaps because they'd had their fill of entertainment or were drunk, by the time Ponpon appeared on stage they treated her with the utmost respect, as though they were listening to the great Hamiyet Yüceses. At first, Ponpon thought they didn't like her, mistaking their rapt silence for coolness. At the end of her song, though, the flowers, four plates of rose petals showered over her head and napkins tossed up into the air proved her wrong.

"It's always more festive on nights like that, with just a few people," Ponpon went on. "I got into the spirit. Since they had not only come, but shown such appreciation, I jumped through hoops to give them their money's worth. That is, I let them have it."

They didn't even exchange words that night. But later,

Ponpon, wondering who had paid the bill, asked for details. That's how she found out about Fehmi Şenyürek. She'd already seen his name on the flowers he sent.

"It was the following night, or maybe the next Friday night. Just before the holidays, and the place was packed to the rafters. Naturally, I was at my most haughty. As imperious as can be. You can imagine. You'd have thought I was Maria Callas or something. And there, in the middle of the crowd, I spotted him. Of course, I didn't know at the time that he was a psychopath – and I still can't really get my head round that. I mean, he was as polite, as gracious as can be. But of course I want to believe you, as well. If he's a maniac, I've got to accept it, I suppose! Anyway, I was thrilled to see him that particular night. I ribbed him a bit from the stage, saying things like, 'It seems the gentleman is back; have you become a regular then?' He shot right back, along the lines of 'Who wouldn't come back for more of you?' He was a real charmer, you see. I was more than a little tickled and flattered. Then he sent a note backstage, asking if he could come and have a drink with me. I had another show, so I had to refuse him. But I did send him my card, with my cell phone number on the back . . . "

Ponpon was slurping down her whiskey. At this rate, she'd be out cold any second. I weighed up the pros and cons. If she passed out, I'd enjoy a calm, restful night. But if she passed out before she'd told me what I wanted to know, or started getting silly . . . Actually, that wouldn't be such a problem. It's not like it was our last night together. She could tell me the rest tomorrow.

"As you know," she went on, "I then went to Bodrum on holiday and to Antalya to work. I completely changed my show, of course. There are a lot of tourists. I had to choose songs and singers they are familiar with. Still, I am a bit of a patriot. I began every performance with Tarkan's "Şımarık (Spoilt Rotten)" and ended each show with Ayten Alpman's "Memleketim (My Country)". Well, not even a week had passed before I saw him again. Once again, he was part of a big crowd. They sat right in front."

As I watched Ponpon I visualised Michel Serrault playing Alben in "La Cage aux Folles". They were incredibly similar. With the same air of hyper-sensitivity, conceit and naïve effusiveness, as well as identical gestures and even the same way of holding a glass. Ponpon was doing a first-rate impersonation. I had to bite the insides of my cheeks to keep from bursting into laughter.

"What's with the hollow-cheeked Ajda Pekkan look," she fired at me, so I stopped. "Anyway, all their attention was focused on me. I was sent drinks and invited to their table."

"Did you go?" I asked.

"Well, I wouldn't say that, exactly."

"What do you mean?" I cross-examined her. I really didn't understand. You either go to a table or you don't.

"I didn't exactly stop by their table. Just sat down for a moment, then got up."

"So, you did go then."

"I suppose I did," she allowed. "Why this jumping all over me for it? If I did, I did."

"What did you talk about?"

"We didn't exactly have a conversation," she replied. "I was pinched a bit, slapped on the bottom. They offered me a couple shots of whiskey. That's all! I wouldn't say I sat with them for longer than any performer would during the instrumental bit."

"Just like you said, they were real gentlemen," I teased. "A real couple of English lords."

"Hmmph! You've got a real bee in your bonnet over all of this," she said.

Ponpon was invited to their villa, but apparently politely refused because they were such a large group and so very drunk.

Antalya! A villa in Antalya. Fehmi Şenyürek. And perhaps Adem Yılmız was there as well. And stuttering Musa was murdered in Antalya. The pieces fitted together like a jigsaw puzzle. But there was still no proof of anything.

They showed up again the following night, then disappeared as abruptly as they'd arrived.

"They must have returned to Istanbul when they finished their business in Antalya," I guessed.

"Probably," she agreed. "I didn't see any of them again for a long time. I had nearly forgotten all about him, until the opening night at Zilli in Istanbul. That first night I found the most enormous bouquet of flowers in my dressing room. It was the size of a funeral wreath. Then he started coming regularly once a week."

"Does he know your real name is Zekeriya?"

She looked me up and down as though I'd said something shameful.

"How on earth would he ever know my real name, unless that Hasan creature of yours told him?"

"What do I know? I just thought they might know your name at the places where you work. They could have told him if he asked."

"They don't know either," she interrupted. "It's not as if I hand over my identity card."

"But you sign contracts and all that," I reminded her.

"For the love of God! Contracts and agreements! There's none of that. They simply count the cash into my hand and everyone's happy."

There was no point in pursuing this any further. Maybe Ponpon didn't use her real name for work contracts or tax reports, but someone, somewhere, had to have come across the name Zekeriya. If either Fehmi Şenyürek or Adem Yıldız really wished to learn her true identity it would have been easy enough for them to do so. However, there was no reason to inform her of this.

Twenty-two

Ponpon's recollections hadn't provided me with much information, but she did at least have several phone numbers for Fehmi Şenyürek recorded in her address book.

The moment she finished her third whiskey her eyes began to shut and she went off to bed. I quietly began searching through her address book, which she'd fortunately brought to my house. I didn't recognize most of the names, but some of the listings were truly astounding. She'd scribbled in +, − and x next to some of them. It was obviously some kind of rating system for men.

There was nothing next to Fehmi Şenyürek's name, and no listing for Adem Yıldız.

I was up all night with various schemes racing through my mind.

The baby poo mask had not worked any wonders. My eyes were puffy from lack of sleep. When I finished shaving and showering, Ponpon was still asleep. I gulped down a cup of strong coffee. Aiming to be as seductive as possible, I squeezed into a black bodysuit and leather trousers. Grabbing a studded leather jacket, I headed out the door.

The morning chill did me good.

I stopped by the corner patisserie, where I ordered a

lemonade and cheese *pŏgaça*. It was fresh. Still piping hot. Ignoring my diet, I ordered another one. As my second *pŏgaça* arrived, Hüseyin entered the shop. The moment he spotted me he shifted his posture. A single eyebrow arched. He gave me an exaggerated greeting. The cur was pissing me off!

The owner of the patisserie knows me well. He immediately understood something had bothered me.

"*Abi* dear, is there anything else I can do for you?" he immediately asked.

"No, thank you," I replied.

I turned around and resumed eating my *pŏgaça*.

As if there was no space available in the shop, Hüseyin and his *pŏgaça* settled into a seat right next to mine.

"Good morning, *efendi*," he said. "How are you?

"Thank you."

"Look, I'm referring to you as 'siz'," he pointed out. His care in doing so was progress of a kind

"Good for you," I praised him.

"I see you're as high and mighty as ever, no matter how I act."

He was asking for it. I had no intention in indulging in a bout of morning gymnastics, but he deserved to be plastered against the wall.

I ignored him.

"It looks like you're off somewhere . . . "

The patisserie owner sensed things were heating up, but could do nothing but look on worriedly. Naturally, he wasn't pleased at the prospect of broken glass and shattered furniture. It was the busiest time of day, and a brawl on the premises was the last thing he needed.

I had finished my lemonade and *pǒgaça*. I wiped my mouth with a napkin. Staring into Hüseyin's eyes, I neatly folded it into a tiny bundle and deposited it on my plate.

"You'll really have to remind me to give you a sound thrashing some time," I said. "Nice and slow... "

"Roses spring up from whatever your hand touches."

He'd reverted to the informal "sen". I couldn't hold back any longer.

As I rose from the table I kicked his shoulder with my left foot, toppling him and his chair. He looked up, startled.

"What do you think you're doing!" he protested.

Without giving him a chance to catch his bearings, I placed my right foot on his throat. As I spoke, I pressed down lightly.

"That will be enough for this morning!"

I winked.

His mouth opened as he gasped for air. I noted the morsel of *pǒgaça* still lodged in his throat. somewhere in front of his tonsils, which were also visible. He was incapable of making so much as a peep. I pressed down once more, then removed my foot with a flourish and a glancing blow to his jaw. The shock had unsettled him.

As I left the patisserie I noted the look of relief on the owner's face. Hüseyin was still stretched out on the floor, looking at me with the same shocked expression.

I had no difficulty finding Jihad2000 Kemal's house. The apartment building door was open. I climbed the stairs straight to the top floor.

The blue-eyed mother, who opened the door, didn't seem at all surprised to see me.

"Come right in, Kemal is in his room," was all she said.

As we walked to his room I looked her over, trying to decide if she would really eavesdrop on him. Unless she was busy, she probably would. There was no sound of a television or radio. It would be easy to hear all we said.

Kemal was astonished to see me. He was dressed in a sweat suit that clearly doubled as pyjamas. On his feet were thick woollen stockings.

"You're early. This isn't what you promised!"

He arranged his hair with one hand.

"I haven't even taken a bath yet!"

"Don't worry about it," I said. "You're just fine like this."

I wasn't sure how convincing the lie was, but he smiled, if only for a moment.

"Yeah right," he replied.

"I couldn't stand it. I'm dying of curiosity," I told him. "Tell me whatever it is you've found out. I'll come back in the afternoon."

"You're lying," was his response.

I looked deep into his eyes. I've always had a talent for staring at the point right between someone's eyes. It's easy to maintain for a long time and gives the object the impression that I'm looking directly into his eyes.

"You're lying," he repeated. "You'll find out what you need to know, and leave. Then you won't return."

I continued with my penetrating gaze.

"Oh, all right," he relented.

"Let's get started then," I said.

"I haven't even had my tea," he whined. "I just got up. I was at the computer all night. I worked until morning for a German company called Frechen."

The Frechen he mentioned was probably the same company Ali had talked about. So they preferred Stephen Hawking to us. I suppose they knew what they were doing, but I made a mental note to hack them.

"You'll have to wait for a bit," he said. "I need to go to the toilet. I haven't even washed my hands and face. My mother won't leave until she's given me a bath. Until then, neither of us will get what we want."

While I recognised a quick mind at work, I had no intention of allowing him to play cat and mouse with me.

"I'll wash you," I offered.

I wasn't sure how the thought popped into my head, but I was willing to go through with it. If things got out of hand, I could always hold his head under the water.

His eyes sparkled with excitement.

"There's no way my mother would allow that."

Without giving me a chance to respond he quickly wheeled himself over to the door, where he called for his mother. She appeared instantly. They disappeared into the bathroom together.

They had provided me with an unexpected opportunity. I quickly sat down at the computer. I calculated it would take more than just a few minutes to bathe a cripple. In the meantime, I intended to conduct a thorough investigation of the contents of Kemal's computer.

He used a broadband internet connection. If I wished, I could transfer the entire contents of his computer to my computer.

First I checked the security system. It was flawless. The security programs he had installed would also serve to cover my tracks. In other words, Jihad2000 himself had in effect enabled me to snoop on him undetected.

The connection was fast and powerful. First I mailed all Frechen-related files to myself. I was guilty of industrial espionage, but it sure beat having to hack the company later. I'd have a good look at all the files in the comfort of my own home. For now, I just copied what I found.

There was an enormous dossier in which he'd filed all the information he had on me. I, of course, sent them all to myself. Then deleted them. I then made it impossible for him to download any of the files again.

Sounds of running water continued to come from the bathroom. I wasn't sure what I was looking for, but systematically scanned whatever I found. My eye was caught by some copied porn. Just as I expected: rough-looking men, women with enormous breasts and leather outfits, whips, high-heeled boots... There was no point in wasting more time on these images. I'd have to find whatever I was looking for before the bath was finished.

A bit of excitement is a wonderful thing. It increases the flow of adrenalin. I felt beads of sweat on my forehead. It was the first time I'd done anything like this. And it was so exhilarating!

There were hundreds of files and dossiers with numerical codes, rather than names. I would have to open each one to find out what they contained. The desk was also littered with dozens of CD-Roms. The overwhelming amount of material I needed to investigate just excited me more.

The water was turned off in the bathroom. How long would the drying process take? That's all the time I would have. I tapped away at the keyboard as fast as possible. Dossiers opened and closed. I couldn't keep up with the number of new windows popping up on the screen. And all of a sudden the name Adem Yıldız appeared before me. I sent off the entire dossier.

It was a bigger file than I'd expected. It was taking a long time to mail. I'd be caught red-handed if it didn't finish soon. The last thing I needed was to make a mortal enemy of a crazed hacker like Jihad2000 Kemal.

The sound of running water started up again. He was probably getting a shave. His mother came out of the bathroom. I identified her from the sound of her footsteps. She couldn't see me from the hall, but she might poke her head into the room.

I concealed all signs of my activities. And, as expected, his mother suddenly arrived carrying two cups of tea.

"Kemal is shaving. He'll be back in a second."

No, I didn't take sugar. She stirred two cubes into his tea and left it on the desk I'd just vacated.

"I'm fixing breakfast. You'll join us, won't you?"

"I ate before I came," I told her. "Thank you. Tea will be all for me."

Kemal entered as his mother left. He'd nicked his chin. The cut was covered with a large piece of cotton wool.

"I hope you haven't been bored," he said. "There's plenty here to keep you busy."

He winked as he said this. His wet hair looked as though it had been doused with grease.

I didn't know what exactly I had stumbled across, but I'd certainly found something. I regretted having destroyed the files he kept on me. He would be sure to catch on. And then he'd become a true foe. It wasn't a clever thing to do. The time had come for a confession.

"I came across my name. You've certainly gathered a lot of information about me."

The mother arrived with a tray, interrupting me. I couldn't exactly keep confessing with her there.

"It took me quite some time," said Kemal with a laugh. "Such a long time to gather it all."

Kemal's mother deposited the tray next to her son. Switching into classic Turkish hospitality mode, she began pestering me.

"My son, you really should eat something."

I was full, but the smell of freshly toasted bread was appetising.

"Thank you, *efendim*," I said. "I couldn't. I really did have breakfast before I came."

Jihad2000 was unlikely to continue grinning when he realised that all those painstakingly collected files had disappeared.

Fortunately, his mother left.

"I destroyed them all," I continued.

The smile froze on his lips.

"I mean, it wasn't very nice of you to access all of that information without my knowledge. It's like being spied on. It's a horrible feeling. I felt terrible. So I just deleted them all."

"You really shouldn't have done that," he said.

He was right. I'd been a fool. I smiled weakly. I tried to look as seductive as possible, but probably resembled Woody Allen.

He suddenly burst into laughter.

"I'm kidding," he said. "I'm not angry. I've got copies of everything in any case. It's all on discs. It'll take me ten seconds to reload them."

The scene had been set. I would have to give another performance in order to win his forgiveness. And my leather costume had whetted his appetite even further. What was my unconscious mind thinking when I selected this outfit?

As he ate his breakfast, he began telling me what he'd learned.

"I traced all those nicknames you gave me to the same place," he said. "I mean, Starman and *adam are the same person. They're both Adem Yıldız!"

"What do you mean?" I asked. "Of the Yıldız markets?"

"That's it," he continued. "And not just the markets, the whole huge group of companies."

"You're kidding!" I exclaimed. I couldn't help resorting to theatricality. I hadn't wanted to be the one to bring up the name of Adem Yıldız.

"Everything is connected to him," he continued. "I didn't even bother tracking it all. They hired me as a consultant when they set up their system. I know it all like the back of my hand. It doesn't matter where he gets online or the nick he chooses, I recognize him immediately from the tracking codes I installed."

"Unbelievable," I said, true to my role.

He was good. I also did consulting for computer systems, but I'd never even considered engaging in such tricks. I've never been particularly eager to figure out who gets online, and where.

"The system is a basic one," he said. "You give each user an invisible tail. They can't access anything without going through the main computer. It's then easy enough to trace them by locating the tail. Easy for me, anyway, not for anyone else."

"What about 'red star'," I asked. "Who is that?"

"Ah, that's a funny one," he said. "It might be Adem Yıldız, but I'm not sure. Whoever it is gets online using different passwords and market systems. I was going to track him down last night, but I had other work to do."

He winked again.

"You know what I mean," he said. "Frechen approached you first, then they found me."

"Fine," I responded.

"I arranged for them to find me," he said triumphantly. "When you hesitated to make them a proposal I approached them directly. I introduced myself. And I got the job."

"Ali won't be happy about that," I informed him.

"You mean that money-grubbing slime-ball of yours," he asked.

"I wouldn't say 'slime-ball'," I corrected him.

"Are you sleeping with him?"

"That's none of your business," I said. "Now, what were you saying about Adem Yıldız?"

"You're sleeping with him all right," he concluded. "Otherwise, you wouldn't have said that."

He was baiting me. That was obvious. He'd finished eating and had moved on to his sexual hunger, hoping I'd get angry enough to smack him around.

"Adem Yıldız?" I persisted.

"Both nicks are definitely his," he said. "I know him. He's a real piece of filth. His father struggled to make a man of him, but it didn't do much good. Whenever daddy's around he's just as good as can be. Obeys orders, tags along to Friday prayers. He's even been to Mecca once. But when daddy's away, it's time to play. And he's as degenerate as they come."

It was all I could do not to reveal Adem Yıldız's tricks in bed.

"You seem to know an awful lot about him," I prodded.

"I saw him at work. He treated me like scum. When he paid my fee he acted like I was some charity case. That's partly why I decided to trace him."

"What about the other nicks?" I asked. "I told you, 'kızıl yıldız' is someone from the market chain."

"And the others?" I continued. "What about 'Adam Star'?"

"He's one of them. But it's not Adem Yıldız. Someone from a subsidiary company is using that nick. He gets online from all over the place. Someone who travels a lot."

"I'm impressed," I told him. The subsidiary companies he referred to could well be Astro Shipping or Star Air. Which meant it could be Fehmi Şenyürek. There's also a chance that Adem used that nick when he visited those companies.

It was clear from his expectant expression that all of his attention was now focused on me, waiting for the reward we'd agreed on. I was considering the best way to either get started or to make an escape.

The snoop of a mother came to the rescue. "Kemal, I'm off to the shops. You're with your friend. He'll give you a hand if you need anything. You will help him, won't you, my son?"

"Of course," I said.

"I won't be long." The minute his mother stepped out the door the glint returned to Kemal's eyes.

"That's not all I've learned."

"Go on, tell me the rest," I urged him.

In order to enhance the mood, I leaned back on the bed,

stretching slightly. I was fully aware that this also had the effect of thrusting my crotch close to his face.

He bent nearly double, leaning out of his wheelchair to fondle it.

"Now it's your turn," he said.

I shifted positions instantly, to avoid his lunging onto the bed and on top of me.

"But it's still so early," I demurred. "Mornings just aren't my thing."

"Come on . . . "

"Just tell me a bit more," I coaxed. "Then I'll think about it . . . "

"No," he snapped. He was worse than an obstinate child.

There was no getting around it. We were off and running. I rose to my feet and delivered a sharp smack across his chops. As expected, he was thrilled.

"Yes," he moaned.

"Look," I scolded him. "Tell me everything I want to know; then, I'll give you a little surprise."

I had no idea what my surprise would be, but I'd wing it.

"Who wants a surprise," he said. "It's better like this."

"You won't tell me anything after you come," I said.

"You still don't trust me."

"Give me a good reason to trust you," I said. "What's with all those silly floats in the chat room? Every other line is a sermon or a bit of Koranic verse. And you won't tell me a thing without bargaining first."

"Just put it down to life's lessons," he said. "You know how cruel life can be. Everyone made fun of me all my life. I learned not to give anything without getting something in exchange."

That's all I needed. So far we'd avoided sociology. So far.

"Don't make such a big deal of it," I said.

"I'm not," he said. "How many people have you seen like me? How many have you really got to know? And what's more, you went snooping through my computer files."

"That's no more than what you did to me," I reminded him. "Stalking me on the internet like that...lurking like a thief."

"You're a real smooth operator," he said. "And a bad actor. I'd expected more from you. If that's the way you want it, so be it."

He rolled his wheelchair back to the desk, and took an olive from his breakfast tray, popping it into his mouth. As he spat out the stone, he began talking.

"Adem Yıldız was at the crime scene for all the murders outside Istanbul. The dates for the opening of a store in Van coincide with Iranian Muhammet's death; StarAir Charter started flights from Antalya at the same time stuttering Musa was killed."

He took a manila envelope from the table and handed it to me.

"Here are the dates. I've even taken the trouble to record them for you."

I opened the envelope. It was stuffed with newspaper clippings and internet articles about the opening ceremony for the Yıldız Market in Van. There was also news about the contribution made to Turkish tourism by StarAir, which had begun flights to and from Germany.

"This will be useful, but it doesn't help me prove anything," I said.

"I can't do everything for you," he replied.

I hesitantly extended my hand to him.

"Thank you," I said. "Perhaps we can be friends. I certainly wouldn't want you for an enemy."

"I'm sure you don't. Because you're frightened. You're afraid of me."

"You might be right," I agreed. My hand hovered in mid-air.

"Get out of here," he said. "You disappointed me. I thought you were different. But you're not."

Twenty-three

I stormed out of Jihad2000's place like a bat out of hell. If he'd expected me to fall in love with him, or even to feel the remotest interest, he was sadly mistaken. By not realizing how serious he was, I'd been asking for trouble. What was done, was done. Only time would tell if I'd earned a mortal enemy. You never know, we might really become friends after all. He had my utmost respect when it came to his professional skills. But that didn't mean that as a man, particularly as a sex-crazed masochist of a man, I could be expected to feel anything for him.

I hadn't had any sleep, and thinking about Kemal just made me more irritable. The thought of coping with Ponpon at home was more than I could bear, so I headed straight for the office.

Ali wasn't around. I informed the know-it-all secretary, Figen, that she wasn't to put through any calls under any circumstances. Then I entered my office. I intended to have a close look at the files I'd copied from Jihad2000.

From the coffee I'd drunk, not a trace of caffeine remained. My brain cried out for more. I'd already wrecked my diet with two huge *poğaça*. What would be the harm in another coffee?

I interrupted Figen's game of computer patience to ask her for a cup, strong and black.

While waiting for it to arrive I got online and took out two empty discs. I began downloading files. First I looked at the file he'd collected on me. Every single movement I'd made on the internet had been recorded. Even John Pruitt! My address, telephone numbers, shopping records, every piece of mail I'd sent. They were all there. Jihad2000 was truly a terrifying character.

I couldn't decide if Kemal was a victim of destiny or the recipient of divine justice. A twisted mind had been imprisoned in an equally twisted body. Was it a case of cause and effect, or did he get just what he deserved? I was taken aback by my own train of thought. I realised I was thinking along the lines of the Inquisition, who believed in burning cripples because they were possessed by demons. I was ashamed of myself.

My thoughts were interrupted by Figen's fuzzy head, which poked into the room after a sharp rap on the door.

"I know you're busy," she apologised, "and I'm sorry to interrupt, but the person on the phone says it's terribly urgent."

"Who is it?" I asked.

"The lady who rang the other day; the one with the deep voice."

It must be Gönül on the line. I'd completely forgotten about her, even though she'd promised some news.

"Put her through," I said.

Gönül's typically carefree voice fairly tinkled down the line. She was as joyous and light as someone who believes with all her heart that ignorance is a gift from God.

"I'm not disturbing you, am I?" she began.

"What do you mean," I assured her. "I was just thinking of you. I was wondering how to get in touch."

"Speak of the devil, they say. In my case, it's quite the

opposite, of course. You know I've got a heart of gold."

"I've got no doubt of that," I said, right on cue. "Didn't you have something to tell me?"

"Why don't you invite me to lunch and we'll talk then. Not where we went last week, though. It was so boring. There wasn't anyone but us. Let's go somewhere crowded. We can check them out; they can check us out. That's always more fun, don't you think?"

It wasn't really the best time for lunch with Gönül, but there was no way for me to reach her otherwise. It was nearly noon and I'd probably be hungry enough to eat something. I decided to forget I'd ever eaten those *poğaça*.

"Cat got your tongue?" she said. "Just tell me if you'd rather not."

"I was just trying to think of a place to go."

"Oh," she said. "Don't think so much. You'll end up losing your mind."

She followed this up with a luxurious laugh.

"There's a great pizza restaurant in Levent," I said. "A real chic place."

"Fine."

"When can you come?"

"I'll be there this afternoon . . . "

"Well, when this afternoon? I mean, what time exactly?" I asked.

"I'm in Altımermer right now. How long do you think it will take to get there?"

"Where in Altımermer?"

"Haseki," she said. "And I won't be coming by taxi. There's no way I'm paying that kind of money."

"Plan on it taking about an hour," I said. "It's nearly 11 now, so we'll meet at the restaurant at 12:30. All right?"

"Fine. But what's the name of the restaurant? Levent's a huge district. Let's not get lost looking for each other."

"Sorry," I said. "It's called Pizza Express. It's right at the entrance to Etiler, to the left on Nispetiye Caddesi."

"The road that goes to Akmerkez Shopping Centre, right?"

"That's it," I said. "Just past Namlı Kebab Shop."

"Got it. I can practically see it in my mind's eye."

"See you later then."

"Hang on a minute," she said. "They'll realize about me there, won't they?"

I smiled to myself. Only a blind idiot would fail to recognize Gönül for what she was.

"Don't worry about it," I reassured her. "By the way, I'm dressed as a man. Plan accordingly."

"Oh, I'd recognize you anywhere," she said.

It was clear that some of the files in front of me would have to wait until after lunch. I had a little over an hour and intended to make the most of it.

First, I investigated the dossier on Adem Yıldız. Even the tiniest detail had been collected and stored. Despite family pressure, he was still a bachelor. He was thirty-one, a ripe old age for an unmarried man in those circles. He'd completed his compulsory military service, opting for the shorter version. After graduating from a religious high school of no particular academic standing, he'd studied English. That's probably where he went wrong. While superficially devout, he wasn't particularly religious. There was evidence that he didn't fast during Ramadan, using his travelling as an excuse. I really

wondered how Jihad2000 had got his hands on all this
information.

Correspondence and e-mails between Adem Yıldız and
various companies were all filed away. There was nothing of
particular interest. He spent a great deal of time visiting porn
sites when he was online. Transvestite sites seemed to be a
favourite.

He didn't seem interested in cars, but had a penchant for
high fashion. His habit of wearing only the most expensive
designer labels probably reflected his upbringing as a spoilt
rich kid.

He travelled often, but didn't stay anywhere for long. After
graduating, he visited London at regular three-month intervals.
From time to time, he made brief trips elsewhere. The travel
files collected by Jihad2000 were a confused mess, and it didn't
seem worthwhile to sort through them. So the guy liked to go
on holiday. What was potentially significant was what he did
during his trips. Of that, there were no records. My Stephen
Hawking must not have been able to get his hands on that kind
of information.

One thing that attracted my attention was his high school
years. It took him much longer than normal to complete
school. But what was really strange was that he graduated
from Sakarya İmam Hatip Lisesi rather than the school he had
attended for seven years. Something had happened in his final
year to make him change schools. He'd left Istanbul and ended
up graduating in Sakarya. It was probably a case of friends in
high places, a common enough occurrence when it came to the
idle children of the wealthy. When it became apparent that
their children wouldn't be able to graduate from normal

schools, the fashion was for rich families to make generous donations to high prestige schools, which in turn provided the desired diploma.

The file contained numerous photographs, mostly market openings, as well as clippings from newspapers and magazines. Adem Yıldız was quite the dandy in each one: buttoned jacket, snugly fastened tie, a raised eyebrow and a pose both casual and haughty.

The only picture in which he wasn't wearing a tie was taken in Bodrum's Mazi harbour, while he was water-skiing. He was wearing shorts that fell to just below his knees, in the conservative fashion. His chest appeared to be quite hairy. The quality and size of the photo made it difficult to determine what his body was like, but he was clearly no bodybuilder. He was neither heavyset, nor particularly thin.

I wondered if Fehmi Şenyürek appeared in any of the pictures. But I couldn't really remember what he looked like. Even if he was a member of the party that arrived at the club with Ahmet Kuyu that night, it was unlikely I'd recognise him in a photograph. I'd have to finish later. It was time for me to go and find out what Gönül had learned.

Twenty-four

When I took a seat in the back garden of Pizza Express Gönül had not yet arrived. I told the waiter I was expecting a friend and ordered a glass of fresh grapefruit juice. *Poğaça* for breakfast, pizza now for lunch and then whatever Ponpon had prepared for dinner... At this rate I would become positively fat. There was no sense in settling for just plain plump. I'd allow myself to get completely obese. I stopped myself. The minute I finished my business with Gönül I'd go to a sports salon and work out until I collapsed from exhaustion.

Newly determined to maintain my Audrey Hepburn slimness, I looked over the salad selections. I adored the pizzas here, but was resolute about preserving what was left of my figure.

I put the menu aside when Gönül approached with a brightly chirped, "*Merhaba efendim.*"

She had apparently made an effort to play it straight. But the effect was still a disaster. The phosphorous green tiara adorning her long tresses was a dead giveaway.

As she kissed me, I nearly keeled over from the stench of the knock-off Joop perfume she habitually drenches herself with. I really must remember to buy her a reasonable bottle of perfume or cologne.

Knowing what she is like, I ordered for us both. She would, of course, opt for the most expensive pizza. A self-satisfied smile was fixed on her face.

"Tell me right away what you have to say," I prompted.

"*Ay*, just give me a chance to catch my breath sweetie. I've only just arrived, you know."

"I'm just dying to know…" I said.

"I'll tell you…I'll tell you…But first let me have a look around. Where am I? Who's here? What are the guys like? Then I'll tell you."

She scrutinised, one by one, the occupants of the three other tables and each and every waiter. She looked each one directly in the eye, and bestowed on them all a tiny screech of admiration. I felt myself redden. It would be some time before I visited Pizza Express again.

"Just get a load of all these gorgeous waiters!" she practically shouted.

Everyone heard.

"What's with the blushing?" she asked.

"It's a bit much," I said.

"What do you mean? Appreciation for true beauty is a virtue."

"Look," I pleaded, "Just try not to shout."

"Fine then," she said, lowering her voice slightly. "You know I've got a weak spot for men like Kadir İnanır. Look at that one over there."

She pointed. I grabbed her finger and pulled it down onto the table.

"He's a young Kadir İnanır. Well, aren't you hot stuff mister! He's a bit short, his chin's too bony and the eyes are all wrong.

But you can't have everything, now can you?"

The waiter, who looked nothing like Kadir İnanır at any age, arrived at our table with rolls and dipping dishes of aromatic olive oil. Gönül watched his every move, rapt.

Realising she was about to open her mouth, I kicked her under the table.

"*Ay abla*, that hurt!"

"Enough!" I said. "If you keep this up we'll be thrown out of here. We'll end up eating sandwiches at the shop down the road."

"What's the problem? Haven't they all got pee-pees?" was her response. Fortunately she'd said this in a low voice. No one had heard.

"Cut it out," I said. "Tell you what, we can go down to Bebek when we're finished. It's crawling with men. Now tell me what you found out."

"You're always so pushy. Questions, questions, questions . . . "

I gave her a long hard stare. She glared right back. Then she pouted slightly as she began telling me about the coroner's.

"The autopsy performed on Gül's body revealed that she had had intercourse with more than one person." Gönül's eyes grew misty as she told me this. "She'd also been tortured a bit. That is, she'd been severely beaten."

"What's more," she continued, "Gül came. I mean, she ejaculated. That was never her thing. She'd never come on the job. 'That's private; just for my own pleasure,' she'd say. She was a real lady."

I didn't ask for an explanation of the connection between not coming and being a lady. She was concentrating on her story.

"They'd also put one of those metal rings on her thingy. You know, the one that keeps it erect all the time. It was still on when they found her and she'd turned quite purple."

Now that was strange. There was no mention of a cock-ring in the coroner's report. Nor was there any mention of the deceased sporting an erection.

"That's not her way at all. She wouldn't dream of sticking one of those things on. She'd even hide her thingy when she made love. She was ashamed of it. So why would she put that metal thing on it to keep it hard . . . It's just so strange. I wanted to tell you all of this because you're so good at connecting the dots. I'm sure you'll figure it out. Just like Lieutenant Colombo."

Her reference to Colombo dated us both. As for the cock-ring, it could only mean one thing: Gönül had been the active partner. And that pointed straight to Adem Yıldız.

"But you're not even listening to me," she protested.

Right at that moment her pizza and my enormous salad arrived. As always, a waiter stood on either side, one with a pepper grinder and the other with a dish of spicy oil. Gönül wanted both.

"Don't mind me," I said. "I'm just trying to figure something out. I was a bit lost in thought."

"You know what I told you about thinking too much!"

And she let loose another raucous laugh. There was no trace of the mournfulness of just a few moments earlier.

"And don't neglect your food. My pizza is delicious. I hope that green stuff is going to fill you up."

"I'm dieting," I explained.

"*Ayol*, if eating grass was enough to lose weight cows would have perfect figures."

And she laughed again, of course. If there was anyone left who hadn't noticed us, they did now. There was no ignoring Gönül's chortles. And anyone who heard them naturally looked over to see who or what had produced them.

We finished lunch with idle chatter. She explained in detail the pain and suffering caused by a rectoscopy. It was dulling my appetite, so I let her get on with it. Over half my salad remained untouched.

As she mopped up the rest of the sauce on her plate with a bit of crust, she dropped a bombshell.

"Did you realize that the police never found her clothes, handbag, identity card or anything else? You'd think that they had carted her off as naked as the day she was born!"

It was an astute observation.

"Maybe the police took everything," I guessed.

It was entirely possible. I've heard that the victims of traffic accidents have found themselves relieved of their wristwatches.

"*Ayol*, what use would a policeman have for the sort of clothes Gül wore?"

"What do you mean?"

"You don't know Gül. She wore nothing larger than this." Gönül extended her hand.

The hand was actually rather large. But that's another story.

"Then they must have been lost," I said.

"All right. Let's say everything was lost. But wouldn't you expect a single shoe, a bag, a pair of panties, an ID card or something to be left behind?"

She had a point. The fact that absolutely nothing turned up was a bit strange.

"I wonder how they identified the body," I mused.

"Once our girls are out on the market there isn't a single policeman who doesn't know who they are. She got arrested and taken to the venereal clinic every other day. Then she'd hand over some cash and get released."

"That doesn't matter," I persisted. "They'd have to find some way to identify the body."

"Then they must have spotted the tattoo on her bottom. She'd had a big pink rose done. The second she arrived in Istanbul. And she always wore a G-string. She wanted to make sure everyone saw it."

I didn't ask where or how Gül had displayed her bottom to the police. Where there's a will there's a way. So our little Gül-Yusuf was even more of an exhibitionist than the rest of us.

Twenty-five

As soon as I returned to the office I called Selçuk to confirm what Gönül had told me.

"I see you've really got involved," he said. "You seem to call every day. When you haven't got any questions you don't bother to phone. Not even to check in."

"Please don't," I said. "You know a lot better than me how the police approach cases like this. No evidence of any kind has been collected and there hasn't been a proper investigation. They just see another dead transvestite and close the file. I'm a bit sensitive about things like that."

"I understand," he said.

I ticked off the things I'd learned from Gönül.

"Why isn't any of this on record?" I asked. "And it really is odd, isn't it, that the girl, I mean Yusuf, didn't leave a single thing behind. Where's her handbag, her clothes?"

"Look, you're right. It doesn't make any sense to me either. I'll have to ask around. I've got a bit of clout with some of the guys in the department. I'll do what I can and get back to you."

"I'll be at the office," I said, and gave him my number.

"By the way, what are the results of the DNA tests?"

"Still too early," he said. "We won't get results for a week, ten days."

"Bureaucracy," I grumbled.

"Don't say that," he said. "I can't really defend the investigation, but we've got a lot of work and not many experts. Unless someone's there tightening the screws nothing really gets done."

"Sure," I said. "And when it's a dead transvestite no one wants to crack the whip. They're afraid of what people will think."

"Don't exaggerate. Look, I'm doing all I can, aren't I? I don't care what anyone thinks."

I recalled that he'd said the opposite just the other day, but knew that reminding him now wouldn't help.

"Fine," I said. "I wonder if you could get a policeman to go with me to investigate further. We could at least have a look at the house in Küçukyalı, the cistern and the garden..."

"Are you out of your mind! Do you really think they'd agree?"

"Then I'll do it myself," I said.

"I can't stop you. And I can't promise to help you if you get into trouble."

After I hung up I asked Figen, whose hair was looking frumpier than ever despite her lunch break visit to the coiffeur, to inform me immediately if anyone called from the police department.

The phone rang the moment I stepped back into my office. It was Selçuk.

"There's something I forgot to tell you," he said. "They found another body. It had been decomposing in the water for a long time. It was a male with silicon breast implants."

The wind was knocked out of me. I'd been hoping that she would turn up safe and sound one day.

"Funda," I said. "Her real name must be Yunus. I can't remember her last name. I'll find out for you if you like."

"That'd be great," he said. "It'll be a real help to the guys here."

Funda Yunus. She'd ended up as fish food just like the Prophet Yunus. But the whale that swallowed the Prophet hadn't touched our girl. In any case, according to the Holy Book, Yunus lived for years inside the giant fish, then emerged and went on with his life. Our Yunus wouldn't have that chance.

I began a rough calculation of how long she'd been missing. That is, how long her body had been floating in the sea. It was months since the beginning of summer when Funda had gone missing. Her body would have decomposed by now. It's true that salt water has a pickling effect, but, in the end, a body is composed of water and flesh and can withstand only so much.

There was something fishy going on.

I'd promised Selçuk that I would find out Funda-Yunus's surname. Hasan would be the best person to handle this. What's more, I hadn't had a chance to tell him about Adem Yıldız's sexual tastes.

He answered on the first ring. I told him about the discovery of the body I suspected belongs to Funda. He'd heard about it.

"But why didn't you tell me?" I asked.

"Like there's any way to reach you. I left at least five messages with Ponpon. I called your office, but the secretary wouldn't put me through or take a message. It's high time you got yourself a cell phone," he scolded.

"So what happened?"

"It may or may not be Funda. There's no way to identify the body."

"But it had breasts," I said.

"That's right. Silicon doesn't rot or dissolve," he pointed

out. "That's why the police phoned our girls. To ask if anyone could identify the body."

"Then what happened?"

"They picked up the first two girls they saw working the street and took them to the coroner's. One of them fainted when she saw the body. It was that bad. They told the police they couldn't help."

"Hasan," I asked, "Could you find out what the last name of Funda, that is, Yunus?"

"So, you've moved on from first names to last names, have you?"

"This is important," I informed him. "I owe someone a favour."

"The police."

"Bingo. That's right. I promised a police friend of mine."

"I'll look into it. But I just want to say something. There's no way a body could have stayed preserved in the sea for that long. The police said so too. It may not be Funda. But don't get your hopes up too high either."

"That is, unless they kept the body somewhere else, then threw it into the sea," I pointed out.

"You mean they refrigerated the corpse somewhere?"

"It's certainly possible . . . "

As I hung up the phone I pondered what I'd just suggested. They wouldn't even need a full-size meat locker. A largish deep freeze would do. They could have kept the body there awhile, then tossed it into the sea. It would, of course, take longer for a frozen body to thaw out and putrefy.

And where are there large refrigeration units and coolers? In the food business. What business was Adem Yıldız in? Cakes and pastries. Once again, everything was pointing to him. Once again, I didn't have a shred of evidence.

I needed to think, but I couldn't concentrate. Images of violent murders flashed before my eyes. Adem Yıldız was killing off our girls, one by one, more methodically than any horror flick villain.

At least Dolly Vuslat had escaped in one piece. I'd have to warn her. It would be foolish to take chances. It might also be foolish to assume that the name Dursun meant she was safe.

There had to be a way. This Adem Yıldız of ours must have left incriminating evidence of some kind behind. I didn't have much faith in the DNA tests, but they could be the evidence I was looking for. How could I possibly accuse him? He was a pillar of the community. There was no way the police would conduct a DNA test based just on my suspicions. I couldn't expect every man around to be tested just on the odd chance he was guilty.

There was no point in sitting here with these thoughts spinning around my head. The files from Jihad2000 hadn't led to anything. Or maybe I was in no condition to see what was staring me in the face.

I decided to go to the gym. A bit of physical exercise would do me good. And I'd burn off some off those extra calories and clear my conscience.

Twenty-six

I came up with a plan that was as risky as it was daring. What did I most need? Hard evidence. I had none. Since it was proving so difficult to find, I would have to create my own.

In a sense, it meant entering the lair of the beast.

What turned the man on? Young transvestites. Would I fit the ticket? No. First, I had to find a fresh girl. As bait. I needed a girl that I could send to him, one prepared to face danger and whose every step I would have to monitor. Preferably, a girl named after a prophet.

I ran through the names of various prophets, trying to find a prophet whose namesake had not yet been murdered. The list began with İsa, Nuh, Lut, Bunyamin, Zekeriya, Yahya, Yakup, Davut . . . Those were the first names that sprang to mind. That would be more than enough.

The most foolproof names were most likely Isa and Nuh.

A potential sticking point was the willingness of the girl to go along with my scheme, but I tried not to think about that. Anyone with a lick of sense would refuse to get involved, but there were two things working in my favour.

First, it would be an insult to refer to any of the girls as intelligent. In the commonly used sensed of the word, none of them were what you might call bright. It seemed to me that common sense and intelligence were not attributes any of them chose to cultivate. Choosing to walk on the wild side, defiantly turning a blind eye to risks, gave us the freedom to behave in an unorthodox way.

I would certainly be able to find someone as mad as me. I had even begun matching names to some of the girls I knew.

The second point working for me, and one that carried with it certain inherent risks, was that the girl did not necessarily have to know that she was being used as bait. It would be dangerous. Some would even regard it as treachery. But I did fully intend to remain at the side of whoever I recruited in order to reduce the danger to a minimum.

Adem Yıldız was not my type, but many of the girls would find him irresistibly attractive. He wasn't particularly tall, but his long, thin face made him seem taller. He had a honey-brown complexion that had looked almost pale under the lights at the club. It contrasted nicely with his dark hair and closely clipped beard. I prefer men with pert, rounded bottoms. Adem Yıldız didn't have one. In fact, his was rather large.

He had expensive taste in clothes. I hadn't looked closely, but he might even sport a Rolex. That alone would do the trick for any number of girls.

Owing to the early hour, I had been unable to find a partner at the Hilton squash court. I contented myself with batting the ball against the wall while I formulated a plan. Tossing out one of the girls as bait could well mean putting her life in danger...

As I envisioned the familiar faces at the club, my own plan horrified me. And the only girls I really knew were those at the club. I couldn't say I was familiar with the ones who worked the streets or hung out at other clubs. The person most likely to be able to help me was Hasan. There was also Şükrü, whose penchant for young girls I'd only recently learned about.

I remained in the sports salon until I was certain I had burned all the calories from that day's meals. As I headed for the showers, I noticed that the salon was getting busier. I decided to look over the new arrivals before taking a shower. I hoped someone attractive had arrived. If nothing else, I'd get an eyeful of something nice. I might even go further.

I loitered in the changing room until I'd finished a bottle of sparkling water. Only two people arrived in the interval. One was definitely not my type. He was far too tubby. He immediately knew where I was coming from. The other was at least as feminine as me. If he thought I wasn't on to him, he was wrong. There was no flying under my gaydar. As he passed, he looked me over as though sizing up a rival. I nodded a silent greeting.

I decided not to waste any more time, and went straight to the shower room. Waiting for me there was Mr Tubby, who was lathering his loins and lardy stomach behind a half-open shower curtain. The timidity in his eyes was belied by the turgidity of his nether regions. I couldn't resist a peek out of the corner of my eye: he was what they refer to as "majestic". Thick with a mushroom head. But he still wasn't my type. He looked at me invitingly, lips puckered into a kiss. I gave him a withering glance and proceeded to a stall as far away as possible. I snapped the curtain shut and stood under the shower head.

When I left he was till lathering himself up. And the curtain was still partly open. He resumed sending me what he no doubt imagined were erotic air kisses.

I could stop and give him a good scolding. Or I could call the vacant-eyed attendant in the changing room. But why bother? I had no time for such nonsense. I still had to find a young girl, preferably named İsa or Musa.

Feeling like indulging in a bit of a tease, I blew him a kiss.

"See you later, hubby," I cooed.

That was it. It was enough to push him over the edge. If there is such as thing as coming over a single word, that was it. He immediately snapped the curtain shut.

Twenty-seven

Ponpon awaited me in a gold lamé turban and my pink bathrobe. She greeted me in a panic before I was even halfway through the door.

"I worried myself sick over you."

"What for?" I asked.

"You're unbelievable," she complained. "Is it too much for you to let me know what's going on? Where have you been? Where did you go? And what about your calls? What am I supposed to tell them? It isn't like I'm not busy myself, but I have to drop everything to try to find you. You're not at the club. You're not at the office. I called Hasan. You know what he's like. He said you were at the office. I called, but some secretary said you'd left. I've been going out of my mind."

She had no intention of calming down. I hung up my jacket and went to the sitting room.

"Someone named Kemal rang," she said.

That's all I needed. Kemal pestering me on the phone! I would have to change my home phone number again.

"He keeps calling. You'd think he had nothing better to do. He sent you an urgent message. He asked if you'd got it. It's about Davut."

"Who is Davut?" I asked.

"How am I supposed to know? I didn't even know where you'd gone. And I'm supposed to know who Davut is?"

"Fine," I said. "I'll have a look."

The phone rang. Having slipped into the role of lady of the house, Ponpon promptly grabbed it.

"Hello."

She looked stunned.

"Yes, he just arrived. Here you are," she said. But instead of giving me the phone she narrowed her eyes and continued listening. Then she hung up.

"It was Kemal again. He doesn't want to talk to you. But he said you'd better read his message. It's urgent."

"That's strange," I said.

"Stranger than strange. I've been looking after your calls all day. Every nutcase in the city has called. It's either the police or someone saying a prayer... Not a single reasonable gentleman the entire day. No one even worth flirting with."

"You didn't have to answer," I reminded her.

"*Ayol*, don't be such an ingrate," she exclaimed. "I only picked up because I thought it might be you. Otherwise, I couldn't care less about talking to your maniac callers. I really feel it's my duty to give you a warning. You'd better get your act together. If you go on like this you're only asking for trouble."

"Thanks for the warning," was my only response.

"I see. In one ear and out the other. You know best. I'm just giving you a bit of friendly advice. The rest is up to you. You're a grown man."

I wondered what Jihad2000 had sent me so urgently. I prepared myself for nothing more than a soppy love note as I turned on the computer.

Jihad2000 had sent me an e-mail under the name Kemal Barutçu. The message consisted of just two words: "For you". There were two attachments, however. I hesitated before opening them, not putting it past him to send some killer virus that would cause my system to crash. I wouldn't put it past him to hack me. Normally I'm not quite so paranoid, but when faced with a certified madman like Kemal there's no being too careful.

I got offline and scanned both dossiers with my most reliable anti-virus program. They both came up clean. I opened them. And froze.

A body belonging to a transvestite singer had been discovered in Bodrum. She was a singer with an orchestra at a club there. Acid had been forced down her throat.

I sank into the chair. My shoulders sagged. My hair stood on end. My mind went blank. I couldn't think.

I came to my senses thanks to a sharp poke from Ponpon, who was looking at the files over my shoulder. "That's the bass singer Davut!" she screeched. "God save us all. I'm next. May the Lord preserve us! We may be sinners, but you created us. The Almighty Lord has infinite wisdom. I am his servant. Protect us, oh Lord!"

Ponpon was clearly on the verge of a fit of hysteria. I shook her by the shoulders and forced her down into the chair I'd vacated.

"I don't believe it, *ayol*," she whimpered.

She stared off into space.

"Davut!" she screamed. "There goes another girl named after a prophet. Davut with the bass voice. He enchanted everyone with that voice of his ... And now he's dead and his voice silenced! I know I'm next. I can feel it."

At this rate she would be unstoppable. She'd been getting on my nerves for two days in any case. I leaned back slightly, gathered my strength and gave her a slap full across the face. Her eyes flashed and she looked stunned for a moment. But she came to immediately.

"You bastard!" was all she said.

Her pointed fingernails reached out for me like claws. I seized her by the wrists, stopping her. She seemed to realize I'd been acting for her own good, and decided not to attack. But she begun rubbing the red imprint of my hand on her cheek.

"You really let me have it. It hurts like hell."

"I'm sorry," I apologised. "I'm not in control of myself either, I guess."

"If you'd just hit me a bit more gently. You know I bruise easily. If you've wrecked my face I won't be able to work for three days."

I'm so fed up with this bruising business! Am I the only person who doesn't go purple at the slightest blow?

Ponpon announced that tonight, too, she would not be able to go to work. Perhaps because she blamed me for her condition, she had no compunctions about taking the night off. My nerves were shattered, and I just couldn't care less either way. I may have adored Ponpon and valued her friendship, but that didn't mean we needed to live together.

Once she was feeling a little better, Ponpon served dinner. As we ate her rich lasagne, and I regained all the calories I'd lost playing squash, we did a situation evaluation. So far, there had been seven deaths: İbrabim, Yusuf, Musa, Muhammet, Yunus, Salih and Davut. As Ponpon recollected that her real name was Zekeriya, she'd once again reached the brink of a nervous breakdown, then calmed down when she remembered that she was with me, safe in my home. I know she thinks of me as a kind of Rambo. While it pleases and even flatters me a bit, I'm realistic enough to see how ridiculous she is being.

As she came out of the kitchen bearing am enormous tiramisu, the final course of our Italian themed dinner, the doorbell rang. Ponpon's cry of terror mingled with the sound of the bell. The expression on my face was noted and understood. She apologised on the spot.

"Ay, what can I do? I just can't control myself. My nerves are shattered. I don't know what I'd do if you weren't here. The devil tells me to go and ask for police protection. Of course I won't listen to the devil. At most, I'll check into a private hospital. At least I'll be lost in the crowd. And there are nurses. There may even be a handsome intern."

It was Hasan. He entered tugging at his loose trousers, which appeared about to fall to the floor. It was no use. Those jeans of his would rise no higher than his pubic hairline.

We shared the tiramisu. He hadn't heard about Davut. He'd learned Yunus's surname. He also said it would be impossible to determine the time of death. Just as I'd guessed, some of the internal organs showed signs of having been frozen.

"Ponpon, sweetie, that was wonderful," I complimented the chef.

"Don't you think it's a bit odd," Ponpon said. "We sit here eating dessert while we discuss internal organs. May the Lord forgive us. If we go on like this we're all going straight to hell."

I related all that was going through my mind, my suspicions concerning Adem Yıldız and my intention to organise a hunting party. Ponpon listened attentively, punctuating nearly every sentence with a shriek to illustrate her terror. When I finished, she pushed her empty plate to the centre of the table.

"Count me out," she said. "I'm already petrified. I'll just spoil things."

Hasan's eyes were gleaming.

"I'm in!" he declared. "I'll do whatever you want. This kind of excitement is just my thing."

"Look Hasan," I said, "this could be extremely dangerous. It means putting one of the girls' lives in danger. If we aren't able to save her, or something went wrong, we'd have to live with it for the rest of our lives."

"I know," he said. "But you can still count me in. Tell me what to do and I'll follow your orders to the letter."

"First," I said, "I need a young girl. Someone brave, willing to take risks and a little greedy."

"Isn't her name important?" Ponpon put in.

"Not really," I said. "We'll make something up."

It would be no problem to invent a name. There was no reason for the girl to reveal her real name. We could even rustle up a fake ID card if we had to. We'd just fill in İsa, Nuh, Yakup or whatever.

Ponpon stood up with a long drawn out sigh.

"Doesn't anyone want coffee?" she asked. "I'm not having any, but I'll make you some."

Her impression of a self-sacrificing mother was too priceless for words. She breathed new life into the supporting actress role of devoted mother, a staple of so many Hollywood films of the '40s and '50s.

Twenty-eight

The fresh young thing Hasan rustled up and brought to the club was just the ticket. His deportment and speech indicated he was from a good family. He was named Gürhan. As far as I could tell, at least, he wasn't someone Hasan had picked up in the street. He had graduated from one of the French high schools, but hadn't yet been accepted into university and was at loose ends. While he described himself as gay, his carefully trimmed and painted nails, plucked eyebrows, lightly pencilled eyes and terracotta complexion suggested he was a bit farther along than that. But I didn't contradict him.

Together, we went up to my low-ceilinged office on the top floor. Although referred to as an office, it really looks more like a storeroom. Cases of alcohol, napkins, toilet paper and other stock line the walls.

Hasan had told Gürhan that we needed help seducing a minor celebrity. According to the scenario, the man had a transvestite girlfriend who was as jealous as she was famous. She suspected that he was cheating on her, but had no proof. She had given him the best years of her life. Yet he slept around with young things, denying it each time. Our girl couldn't take it any more. She hoped to catch him in the act, have photographs taken and then ask for a reckoning.

Our story wasn't particularly believable, for any number of

reasons. We had no time to refine it further, however. In any case, Gürhan didn't seem inclined to question anything.

Hasan had flattered Gürhan, telling him that if he helped us he'd shoot to instant notoriety, winning the help and support of all the most influential and powerful girls, including me. For a girl preparing to make her debut on the scene, this was no small achievement.

Gürhan perched on his chair, doing his best Winona Ryder imitation.

"My mother won't pay for depilation," he remarked, out of the blue.

Hasan and I exchanged glances. It seemed we'd found our girl. Dimwits are a dime a dozen, but we'd struck it rich.

"And?" I pressed him.

"I'm starting to get hair on my chest. I wax, but it just grows out again. I told my mother about it, but she said I was being silly. I want depilation."

"We'll arrange it," I said soothingly.

"And there's another thing," he added. "Don't you think my tits are too small?"

"How old are you dear?" I asked.

"Nineteen."

"You don't look it," Hasam interjected.

"Tell me the truth," I said.

"I swear it's true. I'm nineteen. I started school early."

"You're a bit too young for hormones."

"But I want to start now," he protested.

It was quite touching that he still referred to himself as merely "gay". At this rate, she'd be a plucky little cabaret singer by twenty-five.

"We'll discuss this later," I promised.

Gürhan looked me up and down.

"Why don't you have breasts?" he asked.

"I'm happy like this," I said. "I like being a man at times, a woman at others."

"You look like Maria Callas."

There were more flattering comparisons. Actually, Maria Callas went through a series of distinct phases. Plump Maria, fat Maria; her Audrey Hepburn period with Visconti and society lady period with Onassis, followed by her wronged woman episode when Onassis married Jacqueline Kennedy. I didn't ask her to be more specific. I decided she must have been referring to the Audrey Hepburn phase.

"Oh, and there's one more thing," he said. "I don't do kinky. And if you plan on taking photos no porn shots. I've got my family to think about."

There was no telling what plans Adem Yıldız would have for Gürhan, but we reassured him anyway.

"I've got to tell you something. This man enjoys being a bottom as well," I said.

Hasan looked even more surprised than Gürhan. It was old news for me. I continued as though I hadn't said anything juicy.

"What I mean to say is, you may have to . . . "

"I told you, didn't I? I'm gay; I'm game; I'll do whatever he wants."

I suppressed a cry of joy.

"And there's one more thing," said Hasan. "Your name."

"What do you mean?"

"This guy has a thing for holy names. The names of prophets and saints and stuff. So don't tell him you're named

Gürhan. If he asks, say you're Nuh or İsa."

"I don't like either of those names," Gürhan pouted. "I like the name Ceren."

"I told you, a man's name," I said.

"You mean I have to choose a man's name?"

"That's right. You definitely must," I said.

"Only if you help me with hormone injections."

He tried to cup his chest as he said this, but came up empty-handed.

Gürhan agreed to the name Isa but he seemed such an idiot he'd probably reveal his real name in minutes. We would have to prepare an identity card with the name İsa. Then we'd find a way to get Adem Yıldız to notice him.

As we all left the club I could tell from Şükrü's expression that he fancied the new girl. Our "Isa" Gürhan seemed to be just the type for boys who like girls who are boys. Şükrü narrowed his eyes into what he imagined to be a rakish expression, keeping them on Gürhan until we were outside.

Looking back at Cüneyt, who'd held the door open for us, Gürhan said, "Your barman is gorgeous."

"He certainly is," I agreed. "All my employees are handsome. I handpick them."

"Could you arrange him for me when my work's done?"

"Sure. He seemed to like you, too."

"I know. The way he looked at me ... "

Gürhan's ID card was completely worn out. The PVC coating had come off in places. It was cracked from being carried in his pocket. It wasn't difficult to peel off the plastic coating with the help of a hot iron. Using the same type of pen, I added "İsa" to the name section. We'd get it plasticised first thing the next morning.

The newspaper clippings sent to me by Jihad2000 all had a Bodrum by-line. Our maniac killer, Adem Yıldız, must be holidaying at his summer house near Bodrum Mazi harbour.

We could go there, but there was the chance that he'd be on his way back to Istanbul by the time we arrived. Only Jihad2000 would be able to confirm his location. After all, he was the one tracking Adem Yıldız's every move. I could try to locate him myself, but Kemal was a step ahead of me. He'd be able to determine instantly the exact location of Adem Yıldız based on where he accessed the internet.

I sent him a message saying I hoped he wasn't cross with me and asking for his help. I chose language that was straightforward but contained the hint of a promise. I told him that despite everything I hoped we could do business together, and suggested we may be able to swap work.

As far as I was able to find out, Mazi harbour isn't a busy place. There are no hotels or bed-and-breakfasts. It seemed pointless to lie in wait in Bodrum hoping he'd discover us for himself.

Then I remembered that I did have a place to stay in Mazi harbour: Cengiz's house. The holidays had ended, which meant his wife and children would be back in the city. The house was most likely empty. It was up to me to get him to let us stay there.

It wasn't long before Jihad2000's response arrived. It was, of course, full of protests and complaints. But it wasn't accompanied by a long list of prayers, earning him a point. Kemal had attached a copy of Adem Yıldız's itinerary. I learned that he planned to stay in Bodrum for four more days, then attend a one-day opening ceremony in Ankara before heading to Kayseri for the groundbreaking ceremony for a new plant.

We had to be quick. Four days in Bodrum would be ideal. Otherwise, it would be next to impossible to get our hands on Adem in Ankara or to find a hotel in Kayseri.

I vetoed the idea of Ponpon accompanying us. She insisted, as panicked as ever. First she pleaded with her eyes, then they grew misty as she informed us of how terrified she was for us. There was nothing to be afraid of. We had everything under control. There was no need for us to ask Fehmi to arrange an introduction. In any case, we had no idea if Fehmi was even in Bodrum. In short, Ponpon was most definitely not accompanying us.

"But I'll worry myself to death," she said. "Here, all alone! And the two of you there, on your own with that killer..."

I didn't bother to reason with her. I just firmly repeated the words "no way" several times. She pouted like a spoilt child, her lower lip distended further than I thought humanly possible.

Hasan would have to remain behind to run the club. I ignored his suggestion that Ponpon or Şükrü be left in charge while he accompanied us. The last thing I needed was to attract the attention of Adem Yıldız by arriving with a large entourage. There was quite a difference between being approached by two queers or descended upon by four flaming queens. Hasan sat silently as I outlined my reasoning, obviously a bit miffed at being categorised not only as a queer, but as a flaming queen to boot.

I noted his relative indifference. I've always had my suspicions about Hasan. To date, nothing has borne them out. Still, it seemed rather significant to me that he insisted on baring his butt crack, worked at a transvestite club and had friends only from our circle. Then there were his proclivities for stripping on the dance floor while looking over the trade, his obvious fascination with the ritual of girls who tugged their customers into a dark corner for "crotch control" and his invariable follow-up questions the next day, when he would egg the girls on for the most delicate details, including girth and length. He seemed to be making progress. Now if he'd reach the point where he just bent over and took it like a man it would do him a world of good. I decided to give him a little prodding in that direction at the first possible opportunity.

Meanwhile, I returned to the issue at hand. Our man knew Ponpon from the stage. And he'd seen Hasan around the club. He'd surely recognize them were they to meet again. As for me, though, he'd only seen me in full drag. In daywear, dressed as a man, although with rather feminine airs, there's no way he could identify me. Perhaps it wouldn't be entirely impossible, but it was unlikely. It wouldn't do to underestimate his intelligence, but I felt relatively confident. And I would be accompanied only by "İsa" Gürhan, my live bait.

Ponpon and I had both taken to referring to Gürhan as İsa so he'd get used to being addressed that way. He was as eager as can be, and blissfully ignorant of what lay in store for him. For now, he seemed overjoyed to be part of our little party. He'd been spending his time experimenting at home with any make-up, wigs and accessories he could get his hands on. I can't say the results were a total success, but he'd get the hang of it over time.

I had a ton of things to do. Top of the list was reserving a flight to Bodrum; then came a moment of intimacy with Cengiz, followed, of course, by the surrender of the key to his summer house.

I had total confidence in my skills.

Twenty-nine

We arrived safe and sound in Bodrum's Milas Airport. İsa Gürhan had gone a little overboard in the costume department. We'd had everyone's eyes, and even a few hands, on us since departure. Ultimately, this was a good sign. No one seemed to have a problem with his appearance. Except me.

I had succeeded for many years in keeping my distance from youngsters, whom I generally consider to be silly and obtuse. Now I found myself with a bent boy in tow. I mentally prepared myself for the experience ahead. I was determined to pull it off without a hitch.

I ignored the porter's insistent enquiries as to where we would be staying, and leapt into the first taxi. It wasn't until we arrived in Mazi harbour that I realised how foolish it had been to forego bargaining over the fare.

I had brought along anything that could possibly be of use, and much that surely wouldn't. An enormous bag contained my spy kit. I'd purchased most of the items from Spy Shop in Queensway, London. I had infra-red binoculars, a listening device, and heat sensitive camera and film.

İsa Gürhan had stuffed a bag with his favourite articles from the wardrobes of Ponpon and myself. He'd tried on each and every garment, discarding as shabby a stage costume Ponpon had treasured all these years.

The taxi driver was fairly young. He was on to us immediately. But I was too tense to give him more than a passing glance. He made it clear that he knew the score, but didn't seem inclined to flirt in any case. Considering my mood, he'd made the right choice.

The journey took longer than I'd expected. We were assaulted by the latest pop. İsa Gürhan sang along with each song, commenting on the singers. For me, they were indistinguishable. While İsa Gürhan was no singer, he more than held his own with the radio artists.

Mazi harbour has one of the few remaining bits of unspoilt coast. Cengiz's house is on the far end of the harbour. I handed the taxi driver a small fortune, and we disembarked.

"*Ay*, this place is totally deserted," İsa Gürhan grumbled immediately, registering his disappointment. "There's no one here but us. And Bodrum is miles away. Why'd we bother coming?"

I contented myself with a severe scowl. He went off to explore the house, pouting slightly.

There was nothing much to explore. Other than the living room we'd entered through the front door, there were two small bedrooms, a kitchen leading to a terrace and a tiny bathroom with an open shower.

The terrace was magnificent, ringed with wild thyme and rosemary. The table and gardening set had been brought in. The living room must be cramped in the winter. We'd have to move the whole lot outside. I hate such tasks. I silently wished Ponpon had joined us after all. She'd happily arrange and rearrange a house for hours on end. As often as not, she'd return everything to their original places, dissatisfied with the effect she'd achieved.

Before getting down to business I turned on the radio and placed it on the terrace, hoping to attract the attention of Adem Yıldız if he was nearby. The tinny racket reverberated up and down the empty harbour. For the same reason, we both donned a pair of tiny shorts. I did all I could to transform Gürhan into a sexpot. That is, with the materials on hand, to make him look like a woman. The final touch was an apricot bandana tied over his head. Occasionally uttering hysterical shrieks, we got to work.

The terrace was covered with dust and dirt. We'd have to wash it. I got the garden hose. It was hot and we'd perspired all the way from the airport. I began by spraying Gürhan. Right on cue, he let loose screeches and yelps that would announce our presence to any and all in the vicinity, including all forms of life and the very mountains, rocks and sea. From the opposite side of the harbour a lone fishing boat responded with a wolf whistle. The clingy wet T-shirt completed Gürhan's overall vampishness.

We'd barely moved two chairs to the terrace when Adem Yıldız materialised.

"Welcome."

He spoke in a low whisper. He must have thought it irresistibly sexy. We were subjected to a raffish stare, the look of a real lady-killer.

"*Merhaba*. I'm Adem from next door. I heard a commotion and wondered if something was wrong. There's usually no one around at this time of year."

I introduced myself and gestured to Gürhan, saying, "And this is my friend İsa."

İsa produced an insipid giggle as he scented his quarry. However, I didn't notice any particular reaction from Adem when I pronounced the name "İsa".

"You must be Cengiz's friends," he said.

"That's right," I told him. "I really needed some peace and quiet. He was kind enough to give us the key. There's nothing like getting away from it all, is there?"

Adem Yıldız looked over at the radio as though wondering what my definition of quiet was.

"This place empties out once school starts," he said. "I'm all alone in this big harbour. There aren't many houses here anyway. The weather's perfect this time of year. You chose the right time to come. Welcome."

"Thank you," I said.

"I was starting to feel a bit lonely."

It was time to play dumb.

"Do you live here year-round then?"

"No, I only come now and then."

"Oh," I continued. "We thought you lived here."

Considering the deep tan he'd acquired since I last saw him, it was, in fact, a reasonable supposition.

"Actually, I live in Istanbul. But when I get the chance I come down here for a few days. Business obligations and things. You know what it's like."

"I certainly do," I assured him.

"Let me give you a hand. We'll finish in no time and then we can all get something to eat together."

Adem was like a heat-seeking missile. Without any

preliminaries, he expected our instant assent to a dinner engagement.

"My caretaker and his wife live with me. He handles the gardening, cooks, things like that, you know. He'll whip us up a feast tonight."

"*Ay*, that'd be wonderful," squealed Isa, opening his mouth to speak for the first time. "Our cupboards are bare. We haven't even got any sugar."

If Adem really did have some kind of caretaker, a doorman or gardener or whatever he was, he was unlikely to do much with them around. I didn't relish the thought of spending an evening at his home for nothing. Still, it would be an investment of sorts. And it was true that our kitchen was empty. I didn't even want to think of the expense of hiring a taxi to go food shopping in the town.

"We'd be honoured," I graciously accepted.

The way he continuously eyed up Isa while talking to me was getting on my nerves. But it was a sign that all was going to plan.

As we moved the furniture I realised Adem Yıldız was a lot fitter than he looked. He stripped off his white Burberry T-shirt and was left wearing only a pair of navy blue Bermuda shorts. His body was unexpectedly appetizing. And the little jokes he indulged in weren't all that offensive. I even laughed at some of them. Contrary to first impressions, he seemed almost the gentleman.

He was already flirting in earnest with Isa Gürhan, but occasionally focused his attentions on me too. If he anticipated group sex, he was way off base.

The suave civility of our serial killer was beginning to affect me. I found him hard to resist. He had a charm that was difficult to define. He wasn't particularly handsome, nor did he have a spectacular build. There was no spark in his eyes. His sense of humour was passable only at times. Logically, there was no reason to be drawn to the man. But he was appealing none the less. He had a strange charisma. The way he rested his hands, his posture, the slight compression of his lips when he smiled, the way he became almost girlish as he imitated us, joking around, then reverted to his usual machismo... The man had something working for him, that was for sure.

I may have been able to resist, but Isa Gürhan was clearly infatuated and ready for anything. I congratulated myself for not revealing all the details about Adem. If Gürhan had known, he wouldn't be so much at ease. It was definitely better this way.

Thirty

We parted, agreeing to meet at 7:30 that evening. Adem went home to supervise preparations. We began to dress.

It doesn't usually take me long to get ready. Gürhan, on the other hand, was the sort who needed hours. Every time I called him he'd trill "coming", but remain in the bedroom.

I was tired of waiting. I opened my laptop, got online and went through my messages. There was nothing important. That is, there was nothing that required my immediate attention. Jihad2000 was on the rampage. He'd cracked all my message codes and read each and every one. To prove it, he'd attached a sermon to them all as a sort of signature. I would handle him upon my return.

I wanted to call Ponpon to give her an update. She was no doubt going mad with curiosity. There was no telling what panicked course of action she'd take if she didn't hear from us. My home phone was busy every time I rang. Ponpon seemed to be busying herself in my absence with hours spent on the phone. I resigned myself to a large phone bill.

The house was so tiny it was easy for me to monitor each step of Gürhan's preparations. That is to say, I wasn't surprised by the final effect. But I had to hand to it to him, he was like a graceful, young gazelle. He would have held his own against any fashion model. Swishing past me, he gave a half turn. I whistled my appreciation.

"Sorry it took so long, but what do you think?" he asked.

"It was well worth the wait. You look fabulous." I told him.

I was pleased with my merchandise. It wouldn't do for me to out-dress him, since I didn't want to draw unwanted attention to myself. I chose a simple, even refined ensemble. In a pair of thin, beige cotton trousers and a transparent ice-blue blouse that revealed my smooth, flat torso, I was almost plain. The outline of my white G-string, however, was most certainly visible from behind. That would create enough excitement.

It could get quite cool as the night wore on. I draped shawls over our shoulders.

Just before leaving, I set aside all the devices that might come in handy later. I checked the film and battery, and took the recording device and miniature camera with me.

As we left the house it was starting to get dark. The path leading to Adem Yıldız's house winds down to the shoreline, then doubles back up a slope. It was lined with bushes bristling with thorns and sharp branches. İsa Gürhan tottered along in his super high heels. I took his arm.

The path wasn't a long one, but the deepening dusk and rough track were slowing us down. There were virtually no lights around the harbour, and we found ourselves plunged into near total darkness. I cursed myself for not leaving at least one light burning back home. We'd have an even more difficult time getting back.

"*Ay*, I can't see a thing."

"I've got your arm," I said reassuringly.

"And these shoes keep coming off."

"Why don't you carry them?"

"Are you crazy?" Gürhan replied. "I'll cut my feet. Or at least get them dirty. I can't let him see me with filthy feet."

"Why don't you dip your feet in the sea just before we get to the house. It'll cool you off, too."

"You're so clever," he cried. "You've got an answer for everything."

I laughed.

"But I'm not putting my feet in that freezing water. Anyway, what's the big deal? He can wait a little. It's not like he's out on a street corner. He's at home."

We continued walking.

Adem Yıldız's house was several times larger than ours. Next to it was a huge boathouse, and in the garden a shed of some sort. It lay near the deepest part of the harbour. Through the darkness, I could just barely make out a Zodiac tethered to the pier. None of this had been visible from Cengiz's house.

Some lights were burning on the side of the house facing the sea. As we climbed the stairs leading up from the sea, Isa Gürhan cried out:

"Yoo-hoo . . . We're here!"

He was just like Marilyn Monroe in *Some Like It Hot*. Hot on the trail of a wealthy man, he was at his sweetest and most alluring. Thinking of the film, I compared myself to Jack Lemmon in drag. I smiled.

A table had been laid. On it were lit candles and a bottle of wine. But there was no sign of Adem Yıldız. No appearance was made by the caretaker and his wife, either.

"Yoo-hoo . . . Adem *Bey* . . . We've arrived," İsa tinkled.

Adem's voice floated out from inside. "Have a seat, I'm coming."

"But where are you?" I asked.

"Just pour yourselves a glass of wine. I'll be out in a second..."

I did as instructed. Before handing the glass to İsa Gürhan I came to my senses, and paused.

"Would you care for a drink?"

"Yes, please," he replied.

"Now it won't do to get too tipsy," I said. I looked İsa Gürhan straight in the eye and added, "You know what I mean!"

"You're absolutely right," he agreed demurely. I put the glasses back on the table.

A spread of meze, bowls of pistachio nuts and the famous Yıldız *börek* had been prepared. There was also an enormous bowl of salad. I took a handful of pistachios.

"Surprise!"

As I spun round, I froze at the sight of Adem Yıldız. İsa choked back a half-screamed "No! This can't be happening..."

But it was happening: Adem Yıldız stood across from us in full drag, his arms extended high in the air as he awaited our approval. On his head was a raven black wig. A strapless lamé gown clung to his form, exaggerating his masculine frame. A tuft of chest hair poked out of his cleavage.

I didn't know what to make of it. My astonishment must have been obvious, not just from my expression, but emanating from every pore of my body.

Without breaking his pose Adem Yıldız asked in his most macho voice, "So what do you think, girls?"

"Disastrous," I wanted to say. But I held my tongue. In fawning tones, I managed a weak, "You look fabulous."

"I didn't want to miss the chance to have some fun. I sent

my man away to Milas. He's got a brother there. He'll be back tomorrow."

"Well isn't that nice," was my weak response.

I was at a loss for words. He certainly hadn't wasted any time emptying the house. He was now free to say and do whatever he wanted. Here we were, on this dark moonless night, just the three of us.

When I thought of the Zodiac tied to the pier my spirits sank even lower. I hadn't expected a manoeuvre of this kind so early in the game. I'd brought along a couple of things from Spy Shop, just in case, but I'd anticipated nothing more than an introductory dinner.

Crestfallen, İsa Gürhan sank into a chair. Taking tiny geisha steps in his miniskirt, Adem kissed us both on the cheeks. Gone was the macho man I'd unwillingly fancied by day, replaced by a lady of the night. Even as a coquettette he retained a touch of the thug.

"I wanted to join in," he said. "This isn't something I do regularly."

"It suits you," I said.

"Don't," murmured İsa.

"Do you really think so?"

"Really."

I was lying.

"You know what? I was dressed as a girl until the age of seven. My mother made me clothes. Little outfits all decked out with ribbons and bows. And big starched ribbons in my ringlets. You should see the pictures!"

"So is that why you're a big queer?" asked İsa. "Because they dressed you as a girl when you were a child?"

"But I'm not," said Adem. "I'm no queer."

"What do you mean?"

"I mean just what I say..." he said. "I'm not queer. I just like wearing women's clothes from time to time. Knickers, stockings, garter belts... The feel of silky smooth fabrics on my skin... That's all. I'm still a real man. I mean, I still like young boys like you."

Well that was good news. There was still hope.

"Well, does your family know you're still into girls' clothes?" I asked.

"No," he said.

"What do you do with your dresses? Where do you hide them?" I asked. "And what about your shoes..."

"In a bag in the boot of my car..."

I thought he'd flown here. What was this about a car!

"If I can't dress up with you where can I?" he said.

"A friend of mine took me to a transvestite club the other day. I loved the girls there."

He was, of course, referring to our club. And the girls he mentioned were our girls. He may even have been talking about me. I worried that İsa would give the game away by saying as much. I gave him a hard look. He had other things on his mind.

"But that's like lesbianism," İsa said. "Girl on girl."

"That's what you think," Adem Yıldız growled. He gestured to the small tent springing from his loins. The sequined fabric twinkled in the candlelight.

Adem's taste for transvestitism was as refined as it was grotesque. His mannerisms, attitudes, meticulously executed duties as a host and presentation of dinner were refined in the extreme, as was the way he flirted with Gürhan. It was like being in a well-written scenario for an English film. His sense of timing was impeccable.

On the other hand, his occasional lapses into ladylike manners, the coy look in his eye, his limp wrists and speech peppered with "honey" and "sweetie" were flamingly over the top.

We talked about Bodrum in the old days, how much it had been developed and the fact that Mazi harbour had somehow remained totally unspoilt. When İsa asked who owned the house at the other end of the harbour, Adem used a finger to trace in İsa's lap a half-circle representing the harbour.

"Now, there are three houses with gardens just over here," he began.

Adem wasn't about to let this opportunity slip by. He provided details for every house in the area, groping his way across İsa Gürhan's lap. In fact, he kept his hand on İsa's map the entire time.

As we finished the meze he came straight to the point.

"Stay with me tonight."

He looked from one of us to the other, and waited expectantly.

Then he added:

"The three of us..."

It wasn't what İsa was expecting.

"What do you mean?" he said.

"I mean all of us, together," said Adem. "The bed is wide... and the night is long."

I didn't know what to say.

I knew what he liked. He'd want to bottom. His desire for a threesome could only mean one thing, a sandwich. And he'd be the filling.

With both of us in his bed he was unlikely to pose a threat. He wouldn't dare try anything funny. Instead of ensnaring a maniacal killer I'd just been ensnared in an unpleasant sex romp. I stopped drinking the wine.

"I like you both," he said. "All evening, while I waited for you, I imagined what we could get up to. You really turn me on."

"Well, you're not exactly spoiled for choice," I observed tartly. "After all, we're the only living things in the vicinity."

He silenced me with a hearty chuckle.

"If you're not interested, I won't insist," he said. "But let me tell you again: it's not just that I'm horny, the two of you are so hot. And I fancy you both."

Hackneyed sex talk has always annoyed me. Now was no exception.

"I'm a bit jealous," I said. "I don't like to share my lover."

I said this knowing that he preferred younger boys, and hoping that he would settle for İsa Gürhan alone. But if he preferred someone a bit more masculine and mature, he'd choose me.

I was wrong.

"You'll get a tidy sum for it."

That ruined everything. It was natural enough for him to think that İsa was a whore, but I didn't appreciate being lumped in with hookers.

"I'm afraid there's been a terrible mistake. I'm not what you think," I said. "I make love only for pleasure, not money."

"Me too," he said. "I only do it for fun."

"So do I," İsa Gürhan piped in.

"And what's with getting all formal on me, anyway?" Adem asked.

"*Ayol*, we met just a couple of hours ago," I said. "And I'm not the type to just jump in the sack."

He leaned over and kissed me, probably leaving lipstick on my cheek in the process.

"Well we won't jump. And it's not a sack," he said playfully.

"You've gone too far."

"Far? You haven't seen anything yet," he said, his hand crawling up my inner thigh and onto my crotch. "We haven't left the starting gate yet. Just wait till I get you into bed, then you'll see how far I can take you."

He weighed up the contents of his cupped hand, then withdrew the hand, chuckling softly.

İsa Gürhan tittered. I silenced him with a glance.

"I think we'd best be leaving now," I said.

"But we haven't had the fish yet."

"And what about dessert," chimed in İsa Gürhan, tittering once again.

Adem went to the kitchen to fetch the fish.

I turned on İsa Gürhan. "Try to concentrate," I hissed. "You've got to seduce him."

"But he wants you."

"He certainly does not," I said. "It's you he's after. He's just being polite. He doesn't want me to feel left out, or to get jealous."

"But isn't that just what we want?" he asked.

"Yes, but he doesn't know that."

"Ah ... " said İsa.

Before I had a chance to ascertain what İsa had understood from our little exchange, Adem returned carrying a platter.

"The fish," he announced. "Fresh from the sea. I caught them myself this morning."

"*Ay*, really," exclaimed İsa Gürhan. "Do you mean you're a fisherman too?"

İsa acted as though catching a fish was a fine art.

There were far too many fish for the three of us, but I hadn't enjoyed such a fresh catch for ages.

I had just finished de-boning my first fish when a man's voice called out from the garden.

"Ah, he's arrived," said Adem Yıldız.

Before I even had a chance to ask "who", Fehmi Şenyürek appeared. He set down his bag. We were introduced.

I was as stunned as İsa Gürhan. What was going on?

"Fehmi's my closest friend," said Adem. "We're bosom pals. We've got nothing to hide from each other."

Judging by Fehmi's lack of reaction to Adem's get-up, that much was certainly true.

It was obvious from the way they exchanged glances that something was up, but I had no idea what. Adem hadn't been the least bit surprised by Fehmi's arrival. In fact, he was clearly expected. These two had cooked up some kind of plan.

Fehmi loosened his tie as he took a seat between me and İsa.

"One of our Cessnas was dropping by. I thought I'd get a ride down. I'm glad I did. It meant meeting you."

Adem disappeared indoors and returned with a bottle of *rakı*.

"Thanks, boss," said Fehmi. He turned to me and continued: "I don't understand what people see in wine. *Rakı*'s my poison. Especially with fish."

İsa Gürhan interrupted: "Do you always call him 'boss'?"

"No, my dear," he replied. "When required I refer to him as Adem *Bey*, sometimes I call him 'Sweet Stuff', and then there are times when I just say 'boss'." As you can see, I'm up for anything."

He was a lot more boisterous than I'd remembered, and drunk as a skunk. I didn't appreciate his expression. Every time I caught him exchanging glances with Adem he would give me a filthy grin.

Something had gone terribly wrong. I could sense the balance shifting. Now we had both Fehmi and Adem Yıldız to deal with. The enormous Mazi harbour was totally empty, and the night pitch black. And here we sat with a serial killer and his accomplice. I had no idea how Fehmi had arrived. There had been no sound of a motor. The Zodiac was still tethered to the pier. I'd been a little over confident, and now I might have to pay the price. I'd had too much wine. My reflexes were dulled. İsa Gürhan had long since passed his limit, and was smiling stupidly.

"Adem, honey and almonds," he murmured softly to himself, in what he thought passed for a song.

"I'd like a coffee, please." I carefully enunciated each syllable. "A bitter, sugarless cup of Turkish coffee."

The coffee would help me come to my senses. Otherwise, we were finished. I was still young. There were so many places to go, shopping to do, men to seduce...I couldn't bear the thought of such an abrupt end.

The last thing I needed was to end up as page three fodder, one of the regular transvestite stories.

The question Fehmi asked as he turned to Isa only panicked me more.

"Is your name really İsa?" he asked. "Like the Prophet İsa?"

I was afraid that the giggling Gürhan would forget himself

and reply "No, 'I'm Gürhan'." But he'd been too well trained.

"That's right," he said, simpering. " İsa, like Isabella and Isadora."

Fehmi had a strange gleam in his eye. The look he shot Adem was unmistakable.

"Would the little lady care for another glass of wine?"

The "little lady" Fehmi referred to was of course İsa. The tone used to address him was both flirtatious and belittling. Even in his stupor, İsa must have sensed that something was awry. He refused the wine and took a long sip of water.

"What about the coffee?" I asked, as brightly as possible. "Don't bother. I'm happy to make it myself."

As I rose to my feet my head spun. I sank back into my chair. This was a disaster! Too much wine can make me sleepy, but I never get dizzy. What's more, I never overdo it. Adem hadn't even opened the second bottle. The wine must be drugged. Adem also had a glass in front of him, but he seemed unaffected. Nothing was happening to him, but my faculties seemed to be fading by the second. I was having trouble controlling my body. I wanted to get out of the house immediately, taking İsa back with me to Cengiz's place.

I reached for the glass of water, downing it in a single gulp. As I replaced it I noticed a lipstick smudge on the rim of the glass. I turned and looked at Adem's glass: it was half full. But there wasn't a trace of lipstick. He couldn't have drunk any. The rim of the glass sparkled, it was spotless. İsa and I had finished an entire bottle of wine. And who knows what he'd put in it!

Fehmi began fondling İsa, whose eyelids were drooping. İsa, in slow motion, was making a show of resistance, but Fehmi ignored him. As he kissed İsa, Fehmi dribbled *rakı* into his half-open mouth. Some of the *rakı* ran down İsa's chin. Fehmi licked it off.

As far as I could tell, İsa was in as bad a shape as me: he'd lost all control. I opened my mouth to ask for another coffee, but nothing came out. By brain was working, but my body failed to respond.

Fehmi began stripping İsa. "*Abi*, this one hasn't got any tits," he said. The padded bra was removed, exposing İsa's rib cage.

They were ignoring us now, talking only to each other. Adem pulled his skirt down below his thighs. Under it, he wore a pair of colourful boxer shorts adorned with tiny butterflies. That's what comes of men dressing up as women! A pair of boxer shorts under a skirt like that!

The mind's a funny thing. Despite the danger of the situation, I was obsessing over wardrobe coordination.

Adem slipped his hand under his waistband, groping himself as he watched Fehmi and İsa. Once again, I struggled to get to my feet. I couldn't. Fehmi noticed and turned to me.

"Boss, I know this one," he said.

My blood froze. I couldn't control my movements. In fact, I couldn't move. My body was numb, paralysed and unable to respond to the messages sent by my brain. Fehmi was coming closer. I fought to widen my eyes, to smile. It didn't work. Fehmi's face blotted out everything. He grabbed my chin, turning my head from side to side as he examined my features.

"I swear I know this one," he said.

I opened my mouth to speak. Not a sound came out. Fehmi decided an open mouth was just another orifice.

Thirty-one

When I opened my eyes I was naked. On the carpet, in the middle of the living room, we were all naked. A bit to one side, Isa lay on the floor. There were hands roaming across my body, pinching and kneading. I couldn't keep my eyes open. They closed.

Time was either rushing by, or standing still. The next time I tried to open my eyes I was suffocating. I forced my lids slightly apart. A body was pressing down on me. It was too close to identify a face. I had no idea who it was.

When I closed my eyes my imagination took over. A film reel was passing through my mind. I saw what each girl had gone through as she was murdered. Each detail was vivid. There was only one difference: I was the girl.

The body plunging down the elevator shaft was mine. I was falling, falling for long seconds. I was falling. Then I saw my broken body, at the bottom of the shaft, lying face-down on the oil-stained concrete floor. My body twitched, then was still. A shoe had fallen off; I lay there with one foot bare.

I had no idea if I was alive or dead. I couldn't feel my body. Whatever they had given me, it was sure doing the trick.

I could make out the occasional voice. It wasn't just that I couldn't understand what they were saying. I couldn't even identify the language.

I was being ushered into a car with dark-tinted windows somewhere on the TEM motorway. I couldn't see the chauffeur. I was sitting in the back, next to Adem. It was a limousine of some kind, enormous. I stretched out on the roomy seat. They were offering me drinks. I downed glass after glass of champagne. We drove along the dreary motorway, around the outskirts of Istanbul, from the Asian shore to the European shore and back again, having wild sex. I was aroused by this part. Sexual desire seemed to be reviving my body, the body over which I had no control.

Then the nightmare began: I was heaved into the sea. It was a moonless night. The lights on the opposite shore twinkled like stars. But the water was pitch-black. I was naked. As I slowly sank towards the bottom, fish nibbled, the long tentacles of jelly fish brushed against me. My skin crawled.

I had no idea what Adem and Fehmi were up to, but what was left of my mind kept repeating the same thing, over and over: they will continue until they come. Yes, that was true. Men like that feel pleasure only up to the point when they climax. Then comes a sense of regret, followed by self-loathing and hatred. Once all-consuming lust is gone, the pleasures of the subconscious mind give way to the guilt complexes of the conscious mind. We are of course blamed for what they have been doing with us. They are suddenly filled with loathing for the object of their pleasure. Some flee; others stay, and become sadistic.

In short, time was running out, fast. Once Fehmi and Adem had gratified themselves the ritualistic sadism of the prophet murders would begin.

My imagination transported me to the inferno in which İbrahim Ceren had burned to death. In a broken down building in the narrow streets of Tarlabaşı, in a damp room smelling of mildew and a long-forgotten past, flames slowly encircled me. Then, as now, I couldn't budge. As the flames drew nearer, I could see them licking at my body, but couldn't move. The flickering tongues terrified me; the pain was excruciating. But I could do nothing.

I tried to open my eyes again. The weight was no longer pressing down on me. It seemed like there were hundreds of tiny lanterns burning in the room. Or I was lying just below a starry sky. Right next to me was a body, breathing heavily. I was unable to turn and look. But there was no mistaking the cries of pleasure.

Fehmi and Adem had turned away from us. They were making love to each other. The moans were coming from Adem. His make-up, which had been poorly applied to begin with, was completely wrecked. He kept biting his lower lip, groaning each time he breathed out. He grimaced in ecstasy, eyes nearly shut.

Behind Adem, who was crouching on his hands and knees, was Fehmi – literally screwing the boss. I couldn't see his face, but could tell from his voice that he spoke through clenched teeth. He hissed a string of curses and oaths. Personally, I've never understood the attraction of so-called "talking dirty".

I closed my eyes. Adem's surprises were never-ending. Dolly Vuslat had told me he enjoyed getting screwed. While it was common knowledge that some men requested such services from transvestites, it was rare for a real man to have it performed by another man. What's more, Adem had a thing for lady's garments. And now he was bottoming for Fehmi. I tried to guess how long ago they had reached this stage. It was beyond me.

The pain in my head was subsiding; the fog shrouding my thoughts was lifting. I began thinking rationally. However, I still had no control over my body. The drug they'd slipped me was losing its effectiveness, but I was still under its influence.

Either time was passing slowly or Fehmi was the sort who takes hours to come. Adem was still moaning beside me.

They'd forgotten all about me and Isa Gürhan. Their attention was focused only on each other. Isa Gürhan lay not far off, completely naked. He was motionless.

No matter how long it took Fehmi and Adem to finish their business, finish it they would. I didn't even want to think about what would happen then.

My eyes returned to the dozens of lights overhead. Why were there so many lamps hanging from the ceiling?

I visualised scenes from the death of Jesus, the movie versions. On his back he carried a cross taller than himself, as he trudged up a dusty hill. A crown of thorns rested on his head. Then they nailed him to the cross. Jesus made not a sound as the blood gushed from his hands and feet.

The Jesus seared into my consciousness had a beard and hollow cheeks. His hair was light brown, almost blond. Most of the images in my mind came from the film *Jesus Christ Superstar*, every song of which I knew by heart. It was dubbed "rock opera" and was one of the first works by Andrew Lloyd Webber, who went on to earn fame and a title, Sir, with *Evita*, *Cats* and *Phantom of the Opera*.

Then Jesus was whipped. Exactly thirty-nine times. I think it was the number of years he'd been alive. Again, he made not a peep, while others wept in silence.

The imagery was getting mixed up in my head, with Willem Dafoe intruding from another film.

The crack of lashes continued.

I have a powerful imagination. The whipping sounds were totally life-like.

Yes, totally life-like! I opened my eyes to see İsa Gürhan being whipped. His make-up running down in muddy rivulets, Adem was cracking the leather belt he gripped in one hand. They'd gagged Gürhan with a pair of pink lace panties to stop him from screaming. His eyes were wide with terror.

They'd tied him to two large, antique-looking metal rings fixed to the wall. I couldn't guess what other purpose the rings served. Gürhan was covered with angry red welts where the lash had bit into his flesh. He was trembling.

Gürhan wasn't the only one shaking. As he brandished the whip, Adem wept and quivered. As he cried, still more black mascara ran down his face. He was a terrifying sight.

I was tied up. Hands and feet tightly bound, I lay on my back on the floor. A piece of thick adhesive tape covered my mouth.

Fehmi was stretched out in an armchair just to my right, smoking a cigarette.

"Sodomy! The greatest abomination of all!" he kept repeating. "You've sinned!"

He spoke in an hypnotic drone, emotionless, each syllable given the same emphasis.

"What made you do it? How did it happen? The prophets are without sin, aren't they?"

I tried to move. But couldn't. I remembered, from my high

school gymnastics class, a move that involved leaping into a flying kick from a prone position. I never managed it then. Now, just when I needed it most, I was even less able to manage it.

"İsa died for the sins of mankind. For the sins of sinners. For the sins you too have committed. He died to pay for these very sins."

Fehmi's voice was getting on my nerves. He had adopted the voice of those preachers on television who lecture on faith and the true path. He used the same soulless, flat cadences. The ones widely believed to be a suggestion of the sublime, the lofty mind.

"He will pay for your sins, too. He will pay for all our sins."

Adem raised his arm slowly, as though having difficulty raising the leather strap. Gürhan shook with each cracking noise. In sharp contrast to the prophet Jesus, whose determination to pay for the sins of mankind gave him a certain unshakeable serenity, Gürhan was sobbing like there was no tomorrow. In any case, he had no beard.

"Pronounce the formula."

Like an obedient child, Adem murmured "There is no god but God, Muhammad is the apostle of God." He was choking on his tears, but, as far as I could remember, managed a complete recital of the religious formula.

For a moment, I wondered if I hadn't better recite it myself. I was beginning to think more clearly. But little good it would do me, with my hands and feet bound and my mouth taped. Even if I had been able to move my body it would have made no difference.

The things I was made to watch and the side effects of the drugs they'd given me was making me nauseous. The adhesive tape over my mouth held everything back.

I darted glances around the room, but each time Gürhan cried out my eyes returned to him.

I thought I saw something on the other side of the door to the terrace. It could be the result of the *imbat, meltem, poyraz* – or whatever it is they call the winds in these parts. No, the curtains were definitely not being rustled by some wind whose name I didn't know. Someone was out there.

Someone large. Perhaps the untimely return of the caretaker? If so, he would be sent reeling by what he saw here. If he had any sense at all he wouldn't come in, but would call for help immediately. But if he did come barging in ... If he was a true innocent, had no idea what his boss got up to, he would either leave here a rich man or share the fate, whatever it was, of me and Gürhan.

One thing was for certain. I couldn't bear for a minute longer the sounds of moaning, the sight of a leather strap lashing bare skin, the feel of strange hands pinching and fondling my body. All I asked was that it end. Is there any thing worse than knowing something is going to happen, but not knowing when? I shut my eyes tight. I wanted to lose consciousness, to faint, even to die. Perhaps I wouldn't survive the pain...

The huge shadow was motionless, not coming or going. Whoever it was, he seemed to have frozen in his tracks. Yes, the scene in the living room was enough to freeze anyone's blood, but I silently pleaded for him either to come in and face the consequences, or to run off for help.

It was one of those times when a split-second seems like an eternity. All was happening in the slowest of slow motion. There was no end. The frame remained frozen.

Thirty-two

"*A yol*, I was in a total panic. Not a peep! No news of any kind. Who wouldn't be sick with worry. You have to agree it was perfectly normal of me to wonder what was going on. And the risks you're always taking! As for this one over here, he thinks about nothing but getting some body-work and instantly becoming a top model.

"There was no way to reach you. I waited, expecting you to at least give me a call. Nothing. I cancelled everything. I sat here by the phone. Can you imagine what I was going through?

"All I did was think about the two of you! I couldn't even work. I tried to bake a cake. It came out like a piece of plywood. It didn't rise or anything. And I was so careful to measure out all the ingredients.

"That was the last straw. First I called that man of yours to ask if there was any way to reach you. He told me there was no phone. All my worst fears were confirmed. Well, I went from bad to worse. I was desperate. He noticed, of course. He asked what was wrong. As far he knew, you'd gone to get away from it all, to unwind. I thought it best to let something slip. Just a hint. Then he could be counted on to get the whole story out of me. Once I spilled a few beans he became as anxious as me. He kept egging me on to tell him more. The more I told him, the more worried he got. The more worried he got the more details he demanded. So there we were, on the phone, in a feeding frenzy.

"We finally came to our senses and decided to call Selçuk *Bey*. Of course, I can't remember whose idea it was. One of us thought of it. And would you believe it! It turns out Cengiz knows him. I suppose that's no surprise, really. Things just fell into place.

"He was so understanding. Took such an interest. He's a real gentleman, that Selçuk *Bey*. He said the two of you were out of your minds. We saw eye to eye on that one. In fact, Cengiz was of the same mind. What is it with this determination of yours to be some kind of hero? And as if that wasn't bad enough, dragging this boy-child along...

"Selçuk *Bey* was going to phone you in any case. He had some fresh information. He suggested joining me. I had of course already reserved two round-trip tickets to Bodrum. I wasn't having any of that high-season, bye-season nonsense. Well it's a good thing too. The plane was packed. Not a spare seat. And Selçuk? No, I don't believe he had a ticket. But one was arranged. He is a bigwig police chief, after all. If he can't organise a flight, who can? So off we went, the three of us.

"Just before take-off Selçuk Bey received some more information about the case. He acted as though it was nothing important, but he went white as a sheet. Naturally, I noticed. At a glance. But I had enough on my plate as it was. I pretended everything was fine. I made it seem like I was only panicking about catching our flight.

"He was on to me. I mean, he's been around the block a few times. You should have seen the way he talked to me, so slow and steady. As though to calm me down. I was having none of it. Can you imagine me falling for that? I kicked up such a fuss! Well, he told me everything. He'd received news that Fehmi, too, had gone to Bodrum. I went mad the minute I heard that. I swear, my blood pressure went through the roof. Even now, just thinking about it...I told him he had to let you know somehow. It's not as if there aren't any police stations in Bodrum, a sensible officer or two.

"And then – would you believe it – the flight was delayed. That's when I lost it. There was no shutting me up. I gave each and every one of those air hostess women a piece of my mind, I can tell you. If Cengiz hadn't covered my mouth I'd still be at it now. But then I remembered my blood pressure. The last thing I needed was to have some kind of seizure on that plane, as though we didn't have enough problems. I've got my suspicions about this old blood pressure business in any case. Up and down it goes, without rhyme or reason.

"By the time we landed everything had been arranged. Two police cars were there when we stepped off the plane. 'Welcome chief' and the whole shebang. We were in no condition to stand on ceremony. Just a quick salute and straight into the car. 'Step on it,' I told the driver. 'It's not like you'll get a ticket for speeding.' And that's how I brought them all to you!"

Ponpon's screeches were the sweetest thing I'd ever heard. It was a real raid. Selçuk in front, gun drawn, Cengiz and Ponpon right behind him, with a bunch of policemen.

We were rescued. Adem and Fehmi were arrested.

Ponpon's panic attacks had saved the day. Unable to reach us, she'd called every number she believed could be useful. She had told everyone everything she knew, making up whatever was needed to fill in the gaps. She was determined to worry them all. And she had succeeded.

Cengiz went crazy when he found out my true reasons for

going to Mazi harbour. When Selçuk learned of my suspicions concerning Adem Yıldız he decided to authorise a raid without waiting for the results of the DNA tests. Of course, Ponpon wasn't to be left out. This time, she made sure she was one of the party flying to Bodrum.

That was all I managed to piece together from Ponpon's efforts to comfort me, to calm me down.

It seems I was loved.

I wasn't happy about Selçuk and all those police seeing me naked, but of course I didn't let that bother me too much. Ponpon immediately covered me with a tablecloth.

Poor Gürhan was only semi-conscious. He'd wet himself. Knowing I was responsible for his sufferings, I tried to think of a way to clear my conscience. I couldn't. I took his limp body into my arms and kissed him. Through my tears, I told him I was sorry. I'm not certain he heard me.

The police let Adem Yıldız and Fehmi Şenyürek get dressed. Then they were hustled out in handcuffs. Neither bothered to explain what they had done been doing. They'd do that later.

Ponpon, Cengiz, Selçuk, Gürhan and I were left alone in that house. We looked at each other uneasily. Gürhan sank into the chair where Fehmi had been sitting.

"You're out of your mind!" sputtered Cengiz. "A real nutcase. How did you dare to do something like this?"

I just looked him straight in the eye. What was I supposed to say?

"You could have at least told me," Selçuk chimed in. "I'd never have expected you to do this on your own."

"What if we hadn't got here in time!"

"That's enough, Cengiz *Bey*," Ponpon scolded. "Lay off.

He's still in shock."

And I was.

"All right everyone. I'll make us all a nice cup of coffee. We'll feel better then."

And that was Ponpon in a nutshell: able to switch in a split second from total panic to attentive housewife mode.

"Please," I said. "I can't stay here. I've got to get out of this house. Now."

I was sitting right across from the iron rings. The belt lay on the floor just to the left. To my right, was a tangled heap of discarded clothing. My eyes landed on a pair of boxer shorts decked out with tiny butterflies. I felt nauseous.

"Excuse me," I mumbled as I staggered out towards the garden, Ponpon right behind me.

The tablecloth slipped off my back. There, in a corner of the terrace, I dropped to my knees and was sick. Draping the tablecloth back over my shoulders, Ponpon softly said, "You crazy thing." I had never heard her speak with such tenderness.

She knelt down to hug me. She was so comfortingly large, such a perfect combination of fatherly masculinity and motherly warmth. I wiped my mouth on a corner of the tablecloth.

Cengiz's house, which we'd cleaned and tidied only the day before, was just what I needed. The rising sun played across the still waters of the harbour, swirls of amethyst and amber.

Ponpon made us coffee. Gürhan fell asleep. I told them everything I knew and all I suspected.

When I finished, Cengiz rose from his chair and came close. He held me. I appreciated his doing so even in front of Selçuk. I was proud of him. He kissed the top of my head. His body smelled wonderful. I leaned close.

Thirty-three

We returned to Istanbul. Adem Yıldız and Fehmi
Şenyürek had been arrested. Naturally, it made all the
headlines. Thanks to Selçuk, neither my name nor Gürhan's
appeared in the lurid newspaper accounts. The Turkish police
were credited with solving yet another case.

The DNA tests all pointed to Adem Yıldız. It proved
impossible for either of them to create a plausible alibi.

It turned out that while guilty of being an accessory to the
crime, Fehmi was not directly responsible. He simply loved
Adem and slept only with Adem, for many years. They had a
strange and passionate relationship. At least that's how Fehmi
described it. It wasn't really clear when it had begun, but it was
somehow linked to Fehmi's expulsion from military academy.

Until recently, they had managed to maintain what seemed
from the outside to be a strictly business relationship, with
their supposedly heterosexual identities remaining more or less
intact. There would be much made in the morning of how
drunk they had been the previous night, but that was all.

They had experimented a bit with sadism, but it went no
further than a fair degree of pain for their partners. And they
had bought off their victims with handsome compensation.

It all began when Fehmi tried out Deniz, that is to say, Salih, at the house in Ataköy. Deniz was roughed up. She protested and threatened Fehmi. When he insisted, Deniz fled, falling into the elevator shaft as he tried to escape. Adem wasn't even told what had happened. He thought it was simply a case of arranging a transvestite to complete their threesome.

When Fehmi finally told Adem exactly what had happened, he linked it to the prophets' deaths, and the bloody games began. Our girls ended up like the prophets, and were made to pay for the sins of Fehmi and Adem.

The pressure from Adem's family and acquaintances, as well as his social prominence, had no doubt contributed to his losing his mind. There was also the constant demand for him to get married.

Selçuk told me all of this. Even though it wasn't part of his job description, he followed events closely as an honorary member of the department and the person who had apprehended the killers. There was a strong possibility that Fehmi would get off lightly and that Adem would be granted clemency on the grounds of temporary insanity.

What I needed most was to forget all that had happened, to put it behind me as soon as possible. I threw myself into my job. Mare T.Docile, the account Ali was so desperate to land, invited me to Genoa to examine their computer systems. I took Gürhan with me. Although a trip abroad, girl-to-girl, would come nowhere near compensating him for the trauma he had suffered, it was sure to do him some good. Genoa was also quite close to Portofino. There was no better time of year to visit Portofino.

Even as Ponpon tended to the wounds he'd received from the lashings, Gürhan began dropping heavy hints about breast implants.

I sent Gürhan off to stay with Ponpon. They were going to live together until we went to Genoa. Gürhan didn't want to return to his family. "What difference will it make if I get a diploma," he reflected. He planned to become a top model. I always find it a bit chilling when people so obviously fail to learn from their experiences.

The club went on as before, thanks to Hasan. I had neither the desire nor the strength to face the girls' pestering questions. Hasan would be sure to fill them in on every last detail. Things would calm down, and then something new would come along. Soon enough, the girls would forget what had happened to me. I might even be able to laugh about it one day.

I sent a long e-mail to Jihad2000, briefly summarizing events. I thanked him for his help. After all, it was in his power to crash my entire computer system. It would be prudent to maintain warm relations. I explained how tense I had been due to the case, and asked him to keep that in mind in light of the way I had treated him. That is to say, I begged his forgiveness. In bold, capital letters I told him that his help had given me the courage to go forward with my plan.

He replied with an extravagant e-mail informing me that he understood and, for the moment at least, expected nothing further. What he wrote was a cliché, but the message in which he'd packed every possible example of his computer prowess was truly deserving of appreciation. In a word, it was fantastic. I examined it with a combination of admiration and envy. I still had a few accounts to settle with him. But it could wait.

One of the reasons I spend so little time at the club now is Cengiz. He moved in with me. Like so many people, he has to wake up early to go to work, meaning he also has to go to bed at a reasonable time. If I spend my nights at the club, we won't have much time together. And there's nothing better than nestling my head into Cengiz's blond chest hairs as I fall asleep.

He tells me that I sometimes cry out in the middle of the night. When I do, he holds me tight and pulls my head close. I calm down. We agree that I'll require this kind of therapy into the indefinite future.

We plan to go to the cinema over the weekend with his children. He'll introduce us for the first time. I'm already panicking about what to wear.

Glossary

abi   – elder brother

abla   – elder sister

aman   – oh! ah! mercy! for goodness sake!

ayol/ay   – exclamation favoured by women; well!

ayran   – drink made of yoghurt and water

bey   – sir; used with first name, Mr

börek   – a flaky, filled pastry

dolma   – cooked stuffed vegetables

efendi   – gentleman, master

efendim – Yes (answer to call), I beg your pardon?

hacı   – hadji, pilgrim to Mecca

hanım   – lady; used with first name, Mrs, Miss

hoca   – hodja, Muslim teacher

ibne   – faggot (derogatory)

kilim   – flat-weave carpet

lokum   – Turkish delight

meyhane – Turkish taverna

meze   – appetisers, traditionally accompany drinking

oglancı   – pederast, not necessarily considered "gay" in Western sense

poğaça   – flaky pastry raki

raki   – an anise-flavoured spirit

Acknowledgments

I have always watched awards ceremonies – especially the Oscars – with a sense of amazement and good-natured envy. The award winners invariably present a long list of those believed to have contributed in some way to their general development. It is a fascinating life survey, embracing everyone from parents and teachers, to those well-known sources of inspiration, neighbours and pets.

Presented with the opportunity to compile my own list, I have decided to milk it for all it's worth. If I have overlooked anyone, I apologise for the oversight of my editor and consultant.

First of all, I would naturally like to thank my family: my mother, dearest Meloş; my late father, even if he is unable to read this; my brother, who I believe has always taken life much more seriously than I do; his spouse, the happy result of my skills as a matchmaker; my late grandmother from my mother's side, who was always a source of joy and panic in the house where I grew up; that pillar of dignified calm, my late grand-grandmother from my father's side; various other relatives, some living, others no longer with us, including my aunts, uncles, maternal uncles, first- and second-generation cousins (those passed over know who they are) and, finally, because anything but a specific mention would be a disgrace, my "special" cousin, Yeşim Toduk; my aunt's husband, and my sisters- and aunts-in-law.

Next come the friends I would like to thank: Naim Faik Dilmener, who patiently read my manuscript, guiding and encouraging me, and who is himself a keen reader of detective stories and an authority on golden oldie '45s, as well as his entire family: his son, but in particular his wife, "Belinda"; Berran Tözer, who set out with me when this project was a five-book mini series, but threw in the towel by the time we reached page 27; my esteemed partners and fellow consultants with whom I make a respectable living, for it would be impossible for me to survive on my earnings from writing books; Işıl Dayloğlu Aslan and A. Ateş Akansel; and their spouses Burçak and Suada, who is also my Reiki master; as well as Işıl and Burçak's daughter, Zeynep; and Ateş and Suada's dogs.

Despite their not really knowing what exactly was going on, I would like to thank, for their unfailing emotional support, Mehmet "Serdar" Omay; Murathan Mungan, even if we have not met for a long time, Füsun Akatlı and her daughter, Zeynep; and Zeynep Zeytinoğlu; Yıldırım Türker; Nejat Ulusay; Nilgün Abisel; Levent Suner; Nilüfer Kavalalı; Mete Özgencil, whose painting, into which I lose myself from time to time, hangs on the wall of my study; and Barbaros Altuğ, who somehow managed to motivate me without making his intentions obvious, and who is now my agent and imagines that he will somehow emerge unblemished from all of this.

Miraç Atuna, who constantly reinvents herself and, like me, wakes up before dawn, therefore making it possible for me to have a phone conversation with someone before 7am, and who is also a Feng Shui master and hypnotherapist.

My business colleagues, Kezban Eren, Derya Babuç and – yes, her surname is real – Pelin Burmabıyıklıoğlu; the ever-smiling Remzi Demircan and Meral Emeksiz, who are the most positive people I've ever met; everyone I've met and encountered at offices anywhere, especially the sometimes capricious secretaries for enduring all kinds of cruelty; all of my eccentric former managers and bosses – I have somehow never been able to locate the normal ones, with the exception of Ergin Bener, who, of that group, is the only one completely at peace with his inner child.

And as far as those responsible for my technical development: naturally, all of "our" girls, if for no other reason than their courage and their very existence; my encounters with each and every one of them has enabled me, consciously or unconsciously, to make use of their many impersonations, gestures, styles and sometimes – the revealing detail of a single word.

The publishing house that will print this book, my editor or editors, copy editor, proofreader, binder, cover designer and all those involved in promoting, distributing and selling the book.

The many who through their works have inspired me over the years, including Honore de Balzac, Patricia Highsmith, Saki, Truman Capote, Christopher Isherwood, Reşat Ekrem Koçu, Andre Gide, Marquis de Sade, Chauderlos de Laclos, Yusuf Atılgan, Hüseyin Rahmi Gürpınar, Gore Vidal, Serdar Turgut and many others.

Those whose music has enabled me to find inner peace: G. F. Handel, Gustave Mahler, Schubert, V. Bellini's "Norma" in particular, Tchaikovsky, Eric Satie, Philip Glass, Cole Porter, Eleni Karaindrou, Michel Berger and all composers, in fact, everywhere.

And all the artists who give voice to these works, but especially the opera singers I treasure: Maria Callas, Lucia Popp, Leyla Gencer, Anna Moffo, Teresa Berganza, Montserrat Caballe, Inessa Galante, Gülgez Altındağ, Yıldız Tumbul, Aylin Ateş, Franco Corelli, for both his voice and looks; Thomas Hampson, whose portrait hangs in my bedroom, next to Maria Callas, for his Mahler *lieder*; Jose Cura, Tito Schipa, Fritz Wunderlich, Suat Ankan, for making me feel to the marrow, each time I watch or listen to him, the joy of performance; and for the same reason, composer Leonard Bernstein; Yekta Kara, whose wonderful productions restored the visual pleasures of opera; and finally, on another level, the worst soprano of all time, Florence Foster Jenkins.

For similar reasons, Mina, whose albums I would rush to buy if they recorded no more than a belch; Barbra Streisand, back before she transformed every three-minute song into a five-curtain opera, that is to say, pre-1980s; Yorgo Dallaras, Hildegard Knef, Sylvie Vartan, Veronique Sanson, Jane Birkin, Patty Pravo, Michael Franks, Lee Oscar, Manhattan Transfer, Supertramp, Juliette Greco and, again pre-1988 – for better or worse – Ajda Pekkan; Hümeyra, for all she is; Nükhet Duru, who manages to inject meaning into all of her songs, even when they are rubbish; Gonül Turgut, whose decision to leave music I have never understood and whose absence I continue to lament; Ayla Dikmen, for her costumes alone; and Madonna, whose songs I'm not wild about, but whose existence seems to me to be a good thing.

Those geniuses of cinema, whose number seem endless, but whom I'll try to reel off: Visconti, John Waters, Joseph Losey; Almadovar, for his "marginal" films, in particular *La ley del deseo*; Bertrand Blier, before he went too far; Fassbinder, for *Querelle* alone; John Huston, Truffaut, Salvatore Samperi for *Scandalo* alone, Mauro Bolognini, Ernest Lubitsch, George Cukor, Billy Wilder, Alain Tanner for *Dans la Ville Blanche*, the film I have watched most frequently; Audrey Hepburn, of course; Jeanne Moreau; Elizabeth Taylor, mainly for her voice; Lilian Gish and Bette Davis for *The Whales of August*; Catherine Denevue, who, even if she does age, ages beautifully; Faye Dunaway, before she became a caricature of herself; Giulietta Masina, Cate Blanchett, Tilda Swinton, Emma Thompson; Divine, the ultimate simulation; Bruno Ganz, Rupert Everett; Alain Delon, when he was fresh; Patrick Dewaere, whom I'm actually cross with for his early departure; Dirk Bogarde, despite his having denied everything in his autobiographies; Montgomery Clift; Gary Cooper at all times; Terence Stamp, during his *The Collector*, *Teorema* and *Priscilla* periods; Franco Nero, for whose sake I sat through dozens of rotten movies; Steve Martin, Dennis Hopper, John Cleese and all of *Monty Python* and *Fawlty Towers*; Hülya Koçyiğit, Müjde Ar, Serra Yılmaz – and, why not – Banu Alkan, Güngör Bayrak for her legs and determination; Kadir İnanır, before he gained weight and became thick; Metin Erksan, Atıf Yılmaz, Barış Pirhasan for the screenplays he has written, and Sevin Okyay for her translations, critiques and articles.

Just for being men, John Pruitt, Tony Ganz, Jason Branch, Mike Timber, Taylor Burbank, Aidan Shaw and the late – I was so sorry when I heard – Al Parker, as well as dozens of others whose names I don't even know.

Pierre and Gilles, for scaling the peaks of kitsch, Tom of

Finland, Jerome Bosch, the Bruegels father and son, Edward Hopper, Tamara Lempicka, Botero, El Greco, Modigliani, Andrea Vizzini, Pablo Picasso, before his cubist phase; Leonardo and Michelangelo, for being both masters and members of "the family", as well as Caravaggio; Latif Demirci, who was the reason for my eagerly awaiting Sundays; the Zümrüt photograph studio, whose front window overwhelms me every time I pass it on Siraselviler.

For reminding me, with their sparkling intelligence and wit of the pleasures to be had from life, Mae West, Tallulah Bankhead and Bedia Muvahhit; Gencay Gürün for, in a word, *embodying* nobility and graciousness; and Truman Capote, again.

Finally, and most importantly, Derya Tolga Uysal, for his unstinting support in all things, for sharing with me for seven years the good and the bad, and for his unbelievably affectionate response to my flare ups, outbursts, depressions, fatigue, mood swings and malice.

Thank you very much.
I salute you all.

Other Serpent's Tail books of interest

Adios Muchachos
Daniel Chavarria
Translated by Carlos Lopez

The beautiful Alicia hatches a plot to ensnare the wealthy foreign visitors to Castro's Cuba through an elaborate scam involving a broken bicycle and her voluptuous charms. Taking choreographed spills in front of expensive foreign cars, Alicia squeezes the maximum sympathy and cash out of her clueless, sexually aroused, victims. Add to this mix the guile of her mother who is in on the scam, and the sky's the limit for Alicia. However, when she attempts to trap Victor, a convicted bank robber masquerading as a Canadian businessman, they quickly realise each other's nefarious motives and embark on a misadventure of sex, cross-dressing, kidnapping and death by olive.

Adios Muchachos is Uruguayan writer Daniel Chavarria's first novel in English translation. Serpent's Tail also publishes *Tango for a Torturer*.

'An erotic and brutally funny romp through the underworld of post-revolutionary Cuba...A picaresque novel with sex, scheming and more sex' *AXM*

'Daniel Chavarria's perkily air-brushed version of a life among Havana's prostitutes bursts with humour and snappy Elmore Leonard-style prose' *Independent Magazine*

'Every last one of its unexpected and downright odd twists work like a dream. The core plot of the book, hung loosely around the neck of one of literature's lustiest leading ladies in a long time, remains strong to the end' *Jack*

'Addictive as hell' *Bookmunch.co.uk*

African Psycho
Alain Mabanckou
Translated by Christine Schwartz Hartley

Gregoire Nakobomayo, a petty criminal, has decided to kill his girlfriend Germaine. He's planned the crime for some time, but still, the act of murder requires a bit of psychological and logistical preparation. Luckily, he has a mentor to call upon, the far more accomplished serial killer Angoualima. The fact that Angoualima is dead doesn't prevent Gregoire from holding lengthy conversations with him. Little by little, Gregoire interweaves Angoualima's life and criminal exploits with his own.

Continuing with the plan despite a string of botched attempts, Gregoire's final shot at offing Germaine leads to an abrupt unravelling. Lauded in France for its fresh and witty style, *African Psycho*'s inventive use of language surprises and relieves the reader by sending up this disturbing subject. *African Psycho* is the UK publication of a major Congolese author, named as one of Africa's most important living writers by *Vanity Fair*.

'This is *Taxi Driver* for Africa's blank generation... a deftly ironic Grand Guignol, a pulp fiction vision of Frantz Fanon's "wretched of the earth" that somehow manages to be both frightening and self-mocking at the same time' *Time Out New York*

'*African Psycho*, first published in French in 2003, is the auspicious debut from a francophone author who most certainly deserves to be discovered. It is smart, stylish and plenty "literary"... A young writer to watch' *Globe and Mail*

'Mabanckou's novel...discovers a fascinating new way to hang readers on those tenterhooks...*African Psycho* presents no gloomy Raskolnikov, nor the fixed sneer of Patrick Bateman, but a haunted burlesque' *The Believer*

'[A] very compelling (and very well-translated) exercise in literary voice' *Publishers Weekly*

'A macabre but comical take on a would-be serial killer' *Vanity Fair*

'Disturbing – and disturbingly funny' *New Yorker*

The Bridge of the Golden Horn
Emine Sevgi Özdamar
Translated by Martin Chalmers
Introduction by John Berger

In 1966, at the age of sixteen, the unnamed heroine lies about her age and signs up as a migrant worker in Germany. She leaves Istanbul, works on an assembly line in West Berlin making radios, and lives in a women's factory hostel. *The Bridge of the Golden Horn* is a sexy, witty, picaresque account of a precocious teenager refusing to become wise, of a hectic four years lived between Berlin and Istanbul, of a young woman who is obsessed by theatre, film, poetry and left-wing politics.

'Accessible and entertaining... Özdamar has a Dickensian talent for creating vivid portraits of ordinary people as complex and individual... The novel reminds us that literature is a transforming energy at the heart of life' *Independent*

'[It is] this combination of an acutely observant ingenuousness and a satirical worldliness that gives *The Bridge of the Golden Horn* its mesmerising power and charm' *Guardian*

'Ravishing... a magnetic tale that could have come out of *A Thousand and One Nights*... a wonderfully refreshing book' *Morning Star*

'An unusual book... by turns beautiful, infuriating, funny and obtuse' *New Statesman*

'Irrepressible... Özdamar has been lucky with her translator. But there is also something about the way she tells a story that would, I think, make her words sparkle under any circumstances, and in any tongue' Maureen Freely, *Financial Times*

'Quite simply a great book... With it German literature has crossed the Bosporus – and returned bearing gifts' *Frankfurter Rundschau*

'A wonderful novel of marvellous invention' *Das Literarische Quartett*

'If the world looks different after reading a book and the things in it bear new names, then a considerable author must have been at work... an author like Emine Sevgi Özdamar' *Süddeutsche Zeitung*

'Özdamar glides through the ocean of stories: between archaic myths and modern slang, between inner and outer worlds, between gravity and humour, between Orient and Occident' *Neue Zürcher Zeitung*